**It was a g**
**his decisi**

He moved out, scuttling through the darkness where he knew a deadly snake or scorpion might strike at any second. But venom was way down the list of Bolan's concerns at the moment.

He crawled until he reached the riverbank, then slithered down its muddy slope into the water…and the crocodiles. But if they were there, none found him as he struck off toward the line of tethered speedboats, focused on the machine gunner in the second craft.

The man behind the weapon wouldn't hear anyone coming, but he'd likely feel the speedboat dip as Bolan hauled himself aboard. That would be the crucial moment. Do or die.

No time to waste—the warrior clutched the speedboat's rail and lunged out of the murky river, dark water streaming off him. Boarding took both hands, leaving Bolan effectively unarmed as he set foot on the deck—but he was never truly defenseless.

As the pirate turned to face him, gaping, Bolan lashed out with the long edge of his flattened hand. He caught the shooter by the throat, cracked something vital and swept him overboard.

Crouching behind the NSV, the Executioner grabbed his pistol grip and swung the weapon's smoking muzzle toward his enemies. Every last one was going down.

# MACK BOLAN ®

## The Executioner

# The Executioner
## Don Pendleton's®
### REBEL TRADE

A GOLD EAGLE BOOK FROM

# WORLDWIDE®

TORONTO • NEW YORK • LONDON
AMSTERDAM • PARIS • SYDNEY • HAMBURG
STOCKHOLM • ATHENS • TOKYO • MILAN
MADRID • WARSAW • BUDAPEST • AUCKLAND

For Corporal Loren M. Buffalo

Recycling programs
for this product may
not exist in your area.

First edition May 2012

ISBN-13: 978-0-373-64402-5

Special thanks and acknowledgment to
Michael Newton for his contribution to this work.

REBEL TRADE

Every morning in Africa, a gazelle wakes up. It knows it must run faster than the fastest lion or it will be killed. Every morning a lion wakes up. It knows it must outrun the slowest gazelle or it will starve to death. It doesn't matter whether you are a lion or a gazelle. When the sun comes up, you'd better be running.

—African proverb

I plan to hit the ground running in Africa. I will move faster, strike harder and react smarter than my enemies. And when the sun goes down, we will see who is still standing.

—Mack Bolan

# THE
# MACK BOLAN
## LEGEND

Nothing less than a war could have fashioned the destiny of the man called Mack Bolan. Bolan earned the Executioner title in the jungle hell of Vietnam.

But this soldier also wore another name—Sergeant Mercy. He was so tagged because of the compassion he showed to wounded comrades-in-arms and Vietnamese civilians.

Mack Bolan's second tour of duty ended prematurely when he was given emergency leave to return home and bury his family, victims of the Mob. Then he declared a one-man war against the Mafia.

He confronted the Families head-on from coast to coast, and soon a hope of victory began to appear. But Bolan had broken society's every rule. That same society started gunning for this elusive warrior—to no avail.

So Bolan was offered amnesty to work within the system against terrorism. This time, as an employee of Uncle Sam, Bolan became Colonel John Phoenix. With a command center at Stony Man Farm in Virginia, he and his new allies—Able Team and Phoenix Force—waged relentless war on a new adversary: the KGB.

But when his one true love, April Rose, died at the hands of the Soviet terror machine, Bolan severed all ties with Establishment authority.

Now, after a lengthy lone-wolf struggle and much soul-searching, the Executioner has agreed to enter an "arm's-length" alliance with his government once more, reserving the right to pursue personal missions in his Everlasting War.

# Prologue

*Skeleton Coast, Namibia*

Bushmen once called Namibia's coastline The Land God Made in Anger. Later, Portuguese seafarers dubbed those barren shores The Gates of Hell.

It was a natural mistake.

Namibia's winds blow from landward, sweeping most of the country's rain out to sea. The pitiful one-third of an inch that reaches soil in any given year cannot relieve the stark aridity of the Namib Desert, sprawling over 31,200 square miles of sunbaked desolation. And if that were not enough to give the coast an evil reputation, there remains the cold Benguela Current, rising as it moves along the shoreline to produce dense ocean fogs the natives call *cassimbo*. While that haze obscures the coast, a constant heavy surf draws boats toward land—and to their doom, if they cannot escape it.

Hundreds of ships have left their shattered, rusting bones on the Skeleton Coast—among them the cargo ship *Eduard Bohlen* in 1909, the Blue Star Line's MV *Dunedin Star* in 1942, the *Otavi* in 1945 and South Africa's *Winston* in 1970. Some of those hulks were still on shore, grim warnings to the skippers of another generation, but the Skeleton Coast had earned its nickname from the sunbleached bones of whales and seals slaughtered for profit by human predators.

So much death.

This morning, with the first gray tentacles of mist already

visible to starboard, Captain Jake Mulrooney was determined that he would not add his crewmen or the MV *Cassowary* to the local tally of disasters. Fog and the Benguela Current were enough to deal with, but Mulrooney also had to think about the danger posed by pirates now, while navigating African waters.

The MV *Cassowary*'s cargo wasn't anything exotic. It included lumber, mining gear and pharmaceutical supplies—any of which might draw the interest of a pirate crew while they were churning north from Cape Town toward another pickup at Port Harcourt before they started the long westward haul toward the States. Reported incidents of piracy were escalating everywhere along the coast of Africa, and while Namibia still couldn't hold a candle to the mayhem of anarchic Somalia, it was catching up.

More fog ahead, driven by winds from shore. Captain Mulrooney was about to issue orders for a change of course, putting more space between the MV *Cassowary* and the coastline, when his first mate, Don Kincaid, spoke softly, urgently.

"We have a bogey on the radar, sir," he said. "Approaching from the northwest at a speed of thirty-five knots. Collision course, unless they spot us and veer off."

Thirty-five knots was translated to forty miles per hour in landlubber's terms, a respectable pace when compared to the MV *Cassowary*'s top speed of twenty knots. The unknown craft could overtake them from behind with no great effort, and approaching from the bow, to cut across their path, the intercept was guaranteed.

Coincidence? A boater out for sportfishing or laughs, who hadn't seen the MV *Cassowary* yet? Maybe. But Mulrooney couldn't stake his life and cargo on a theory of coincidence.

"How long to contact at our present speed?" the captain asked.

"I make it thirteen minutes, sir," the mate replied.

"Hail them and ask for an ID," Mulrooney ordered.

"Aye, sir."

Staring into mist and spitting rain with Zeiss binoculars,

Mulrooney listened while Kincaid broadcast the call. He was disturbed, but not surprised, when no reply came through the speakers mounted on the MV *Cassowary*'s bridge. Another try; the same result.

Kincaid stated the obvious. "They're running silent, sir."

"Okay," Mulrooney said. "Identify us one more time, alert them that they're traveling on a collision course...and warn them that we're armed."

Kincaid frowned at the order but acknowledged it, and did as he was told.

The MV *Cassowary* was a merchant vessel, not a battle wagon, but that didn't mean she was defenseless. Any captain sailing into so-called third-world waters without guns and ammunition stashed aboard these days would rate the designation of a world-class idiot.

When Kincaid's warning brought no answer from the smaller, faster craft, Captain Mulrooney said, "Break out the hardware, Don. All hands to duty stations, just in case."

"Aye, sir!"

The hardware came to half a dozen 12-gauge riot shotguns, one semiautomatic AR-15 rifle and Mulrooney's .45-caliber Colt Combat Commander. None of the crew was trained in handling firearms, as far as Mulrooney knew, but how much skill did it take to point and fire a shotgun at close range?

There'd be no shooting, anyway, unless the MV *Cassowary* was attacked. In that case, he and Kincaid would try to block any attempted boarding. Failing that...well, they could turn the ship into a floating Alamo, if need be, but Mulrooney prayed it wouldn't come to that.

The trouble these days was that you could never trust a pirate gang to loot a ship and leave, or even take the craft and put its crew ashore. At last count, according to the International Maritime Bureau, pirates in Somalia alone had been holding more than five hundred hostages, demanding ransom from the owners of their vessels under threat of death.

And Mulrooney wasn't winding up that way.

Not while he had a trigger finger left.

"Visual contact, sir," Kincaid said.

Mulrooney found the strange boat with his glasses, spotted the armed men along its rails. His stomach tightened, hit him with a sudden rush of unaccustomed nausea. Mulrooney fought it down and told his crewmen on the bridge, "We won't be stopping. If they try to board, they'll have to do it at top speed and under fire. Worse comes to worst, we ram them. Leave them sinking."

"Aye, sir!" came the chorus from his men.

They seemed almost exuberant, as if it was some kind of game. Damned youngsters, raised in video arcades where players gunned down everything from gangbangers and cops to alien invaders with no consequence besides the loss of pocket change. It shouldn't be that easy—and it wasn't, in real life, as Jake Mulrooney had discovered during Operation Desert Storm. The trick to surviving a firefight was—

"Sir!" Kincaid's tone quickly focused the captain's attention. "They seem to have some kind of rocket launcher."

"That's an RPG," Mulrooney said, as he observed the pirate at the speedboat's prow. "Rocket-propelled grenade."

Call it the modern version of your grandfather's bazooka or the German *Panzerfäust* from the Second World War. He couldn't judge the warhead's size or nomenclature from the MV *Cassowary*'s bridge, but if they scored a hit....

"Firing!" Kincaid announced, as if they needed any kind of play-by-play. There were no blind men on the bridge. All of them saw the RPG's back blast, had time to note that it had scorched the small attack craft's forward deck, and then it was a scramble for the nearest cover as the rocket hurtled toward them, riding on a tail of flame.

*A damned good shot,* Mulrooney thought, with grudging admiration, as the RPG came home, smashed through the window he'd been peering from a moment earlier, and detonated as it struck the bulkhead opposite. The blast ruptured his eardrums, deafened him forever, and he saw the fireball coming for him, even with his eyes pressed tightly shut.

Too late to fight.

*So this is what it's like,* Mulrooney thought, *to go down with the ship.*

*Durissa Bay, Namibia*

The soldier came ashore by moonlight, solo, powering a nine-foot Zodiac inflatable by the strength of arms and back alone, its outboard motor shipped and silent. He made no more sound emerging from the water than a fish might while leaping for an insect lit by starshine in the night. No one observed him. No one heard.

Mack Bolan dragged the Zodiac above the waterline and stashed it in a patch of six-foot-tall kunai grass where it would likely pass unnoticed, barring a determined search. He thought of wiping out the drag marks leading from the surf, but then decided it would be a waste of time.

The men he'd come for did not ordinarily patrol the beach. They might have lookouts closer to their camp—in fact, he would be counting on it—but the compound lay a mile or better from the spot where Bolan stood beside his Zodiac, breathing the scents of Africa.

Some scholars said it was the cradle of humanity. Bolan had not studied enough on that score to debate it, one way or another, but he knew that a lot of what he'd seen in Africa during his several tours of duty on the continent was inhumane. From slavery and genocide, to tribal warfare that persisted over centuries, cruel exploitation by imperial invaders, rape of the environment for profit, famine, epidemics, revolution, terrorism—Africa had seen it all.

And most of it was still continuing, to this day.

Bolan's concern, this night, involved a band of pirates operating out of Durissa Bay. They were earmarked as his entry point for a campaign designed to reach beyond their local stronghold into quarters where a combination of corruption and extremist zeal made life more dangerous than it had any need to be.

Bolan was dressed in digicam—the digital camouflage pattern adopted for U.S. Army uniforms in 2004—with war paint to match on his face and his hands. Tan rough-out desert boots and moisture-wicking socks protected his feet. His web gear was the "Molly" setup—MOLLE, for MOdular Lightweight Load-carrying Equipment—that had replaced Vietnam-era "Alice" rigging in recent years.

His weapons were the basics for a job on foreign soil. To accommodate the local trend in ammunition for assault rifles, he'd picked an AK-47 rifle that was standard-issue for the Namibia Defense Force, chambered in 7.62x39 mm. The GP-30 grenade launcher attached beneath its barrel added three pounds to the weapon and fired 40 mm caseless rounds. Native soldiers and police used a variety of semiauto sidearms chambered for 9x19 mm Parabellum bullets, so Bolan had chosen a Beretta 92-FS to fill his holster, its muzzle threaded to accept a sound-suppressor. When it came to cutting, he had gone old-school, selecting a classic Mark I trench knife with a blackened double-edged blade and spiked brass knuckles on the grip. Aside from the GP-30's caseless HE rounds, he also carried Russian RGN fragmentation grenades—short for *Ruchnaya Granata Nastupatel'naya*—with a kill radius of between twenty and sixty-six feet and dual fuses for detonation on impact or after elapse of four seconds, whichever came first.

Because he couldn't trust the moonlight on a night with scudding clouds, Bolan also wore a pair of lightweight LUCIE night-vision goggles that turned the landscape in front of him an eerie green. Manufactured in Germany, where night-vision devices had been pioneered during the Second World War, the fourth-generation headgear offered a crystal-clear view of the beach and the river that Bolan would be following on foot to reach his target.

After a quick stop to make last-minute preparations on the river's southern bank.

Wildlife did not concern Bolan as he moved inland. The largest four-legged predators in residence were brown hyenas, shy of men unless they caught them sleeping in the open and could bite a face off in a rush. He did keep an eye on the ground for puff adders and cobras, but met no reptiles on his way to the river. Once there, he gave a thought to crocodiles, but, with his LUCIE goggles, saw none lurking on the bank or in the water.

He was good to go.

A mile or less in front of him, the district's most ferocious predators had no idea they were about to host a visit from The Executioner.

JACKSON ANDJABA HAD not planned to be a criminal when he was growing up. A member of the Himba tribe, born in the Kunene Region of northwestern Namibia, he had quickly tired of tending goats and cattle in a hamlet consisting of round thatched huts. At fifteen, he had fled the village for a town of some twelve thousand souls, Opuwo, but it had still seemed too small for him. Another year had found him in the capital, Windhoek, with twenty times Opuwo's population and no end of opportunities for a young man.

Or so it seemed, at first.

Andjaba had discovered that his rural background and his relative naïvete made him unsuited for survival in the city. He had learned that friends were vital, and had found them where he could, among the young and tough slumdwellers scrabbling to exist from day to day. In their society, no stigma was attached to theft or acts of violence broadly defined as self-defense. The missionaries who had visited his childhood village in Kunene had it wrong. The Golden Rule should read: unto others first, and do it right the first time.

His first killing had been accidental, grappling for a knife an enemy had planned to gut him with, but it secured Andjaba's reputation as a fighter who would go the limit, no holds barred. He graduated after that to more elaborate and dangerous conspiracies—hijackings, home invasions, theft of arms from military transports. Soon, he was recruited by a mixed troop of Angolan exiles and Namibians who liked a little revolutionary politics mixed with their looting.

Perfect.

It pleased him to go sailing on the ocean he had never seen until his twenty-second birthday, and while doing so, to terrorize the high and mighty captains with their cargos bound for places he would never visit, meant for selling on behalf of masters who already had more money than their great-grandchildren's grandchildren could ever spend. It made him feel…significant.

Andjaba still preferred the city life, but he endured the camp behind Durissa Bay because it was his first full-fledged command, located midway between Ugabmond and Bandombaai, two coastal fishing villages where the young women were impressed by men with guns and money, while their elders understood the risks involved in any protest. No one dared speak to the authorities, since Andjaba had removed the nosy mayor of Ugabmond and dropped him down a dry well in the desert, where his bones would lie until the end of days.

In theory, Andjaba and his men were hunted by the army and Namibia Police Service, but neither seemed to have much luck locating them. In part, he knew that was because of bribes paid to authorities in Windhoek. On the other hand, he knew that some of those in power also sympathized with the Angolan refugees who led the movement that Andjaba served. Drawn by the lures of politics and profit, men often behaved in unexpected ways.

They would go raiding once again tomorrow, when a British oil tanker was scheduled to be passing by. Its course was set from Lagos, for the pickup, to delivery at the SAPREF refinery, ten miles below Durban, South Africa. The ship was a VLCC—Very Large Crude Carrier—still smaller than the ultra-large ULCCs, but capable of loading 320,000 deadweight tonnage. New, the tanker cost around $120 million, while its cargo—or the threat of spilling it at sea—was vastly greater.

In the morning, early, they would—

The explosion shocked Andjaba so much that he dropped his bottle of Tafel lager, half-full, and nearly fell off his camp chair. Someone screamed, a drawn-out cry of agony, that sent Andjaba scrambling for his rifle, feeling panic clamp its grip around his heart.

BOLAN HAD FOUND ONE sentry lounging on an overlook, along the river's southern bank, apparently convinced the compound he'd been set to guard was out of bounds for any adversary. By the time he recognized that critical mistake, he had forgotten how to breathe, the process interrupted by the blade of Bolan's Mark I severing his larynx and carotid arteries. The young man couldn't whimper, but he spluttered for a bit before he died.

In passing, Bolan claimed the 40-round detachable box magazine from his first kill's Kalashnikov, and two more thirties from his saggy pockets. Done with that, he pitched the empty AK down the river's bank and watched it vanish with a muffled splash. There was no point in leaving guns behind that might be used by enemies to kill him, and the extra ammo might be useful, too.

If he'd had all the bullets in the world, it might have been a safer place.

Closing on the pirate camp, Bolan could hear the normal sounds of men conversing, doing chores, bitching about the work. Something was cooking, but he couldn't place the smell. Some kind of bushmeat he supposed, and put it out of mind. Whatever they had in the pot, these murderers and poachers were about to miss their final meal on Earth.

Bolan had primed his GP-30 launcher with a high-explosive caseless round before he left the Zodiac inflatable. He'd heard Russian soldiers called the weapon *Obuvka* (shoe), while dubbing its predecessor models *Kostyor* (bonfire) and *Mukha* (fly). All three were single-shot muzzle-loaders, chambered for the 40x46 mm low-velocity grenades designed for hand-held launchers, rather than the 40x53 mm rounds fired from mounted or crew-served weapons. You could mistake them at a glance, but that mistake would cost a careless warrior dearly—as in hands, eyes or his life.

Today, Bolan's "shoe" was loaded with a VOG-25P fragmentation grenade, average kill radius twenty feet. The projectile's warhead contained thirty-seven grams of TNT, plus a primary charge that bounced it anywhere from three to six feet off the ground before the main charge blew. It was a "Bouncing Betty" for the new millennium, designed to make the art of killing more efficient.

Just what Bolan needed here—at this time.

The pirates—some of them Namibian, the rest Angolan refugees—had four boats moored along the river, with their tents set back some distance from the water's edge. It could have passed for a large safari's camp, until you saw the automatic weapons everywhere and noticed that the men in camp all wore tricolor armbands: red, black and yellow, with a red star on the center stripe.

Small versions of a banner flown by the Mayombe Liberation Front.

The GP-30 had sights adjustable to thirteen hundred feet—call it four football fields and change—but Bolan was within one-quarter of that distance when he chose his target, picking out the farthest boat from where he stood in shadow, half a dozen men engaged in working on its motor. When he fired, the AK-47 barely kicked against his shoulder, and the launcher made a muffled *pop* that could have been mistaken for a normal sound around the camp.

Until his fragmentation round went off.

Four men went down in the initial blast, shot through with shrapnel, dead or gravely wounded as they fell. Two others suffered deep flesh wounds but managed to escape under their own power, diving for weapons they had laid aside when they took up their wrenches, screwdrivers and other tools.

The screaming started then, Bolan deliberately deaf to it as he advanced, using the forest near the river to conceal himself. A mile or so to the north or south, and he'd have been exposed to view as he crossed desert sand, but there was shade and shelter at the riverside for pirates and the man who hunted them.

The hunt was on, and it would not end until all of them were dead.

JACKSON ANDJABA SCANNED the treeline, searching for the enemy who had discharged the blast among his men. He'd recognized the sound of the grenade launcher—most of the weapons issued to Namibia's armed forces had been made in Russia, after all—but one pop did not help him place the shooter, and the detonation told him only that the camp was under fire.

Not from the army, though. Andjaba knew that if a team of soldiers had been sent against them, they'd be charging from the forest already, spraying the camp with automatic weapons, shouting for surrender even as they shot his scrambling men without remorse. War in Namibia had never been an exercise in surgical precision. Winners claimed their victory by standing on a heap of corpses, satisfied that no one had survived to challenge them.

Andjaba shouted orders at his men: the obvious, commanding that they look for cover, watch the trees, control their fire until they had a target. They were well supplied with ammunition, but could not afford to waste it blasting trees and shadows while their adversaries used the night against them as a weapon.

"Douse that fire!" Andjaba bellowed. "And those torches! Keep your damned heads down!"

He heard another pop, and braced himself for the explosion that he knew was coming, no way to prepare for it or save himself except by dropping prone with arms over his head.

More screams followed the detonation, and his men were firing now without a trace of discipline, spraying the night with their Kalashnikovs, one blasting with the NSV heavy machine gun mounted on the second boat in line, shredding the darkness with its muzzle-flashes and its 12.7x108 mm rounds. One in every seven bullets was a tracer, drawing ruby arcs across the weapon's field of fire.

Seen from a distant bird's-eye view, the camp might have appeared to be engaged in a frenetic celebration, but it was hell at ground level and getting worse by the second. Andjaba's soldiers couldn't hope to hear him now over the racket of their guns. And what would he have told them anyway? Keep firing? Cut and run? Offer a prayer to gods they'd long forgotten and ignored?

Crawling on his belly like a lizard, any trace of pride abandoned in that moment on the killing ground, Andjaba searched the treeline for a muzzle-flash that would betray one of their enemies. He could not separate incoming fire from that which his men were laying down, but after seeing first one pirate drop, and then another, he knew that the enemy was using something besides just grenades.

Where *were* they? How had they approached to killing range without a warning from the guard he'd posted on the river?

That was easy. They had killed the lookout, young Paolo Alves, without making any fuss about it. Andjaba would find his body later, if he managed to survive the trap that had been sprung against him. In the meantime, though, survival was his top priority.

Survival, and elimination of his foes.

Or was it wiser to attempt escape?

Three of their boats were still unharmed. If he could rally his surviving men in time to board and flee, their enemies—who clearly had approached on foot somehow—could only stand and watch them disappear into the night. The river flowed another fifty, maybe sixty miles inland, to Lake Mbuende. He could ditch the boats there and lead his people overland, a forced march to the nearest town, where they could pick up any vehicles available and make good their escape.

But first, he needed some way to communicate amidst the hellish racket in the compound. Some way to reassert command and turn his panicked men into a fighting force once more.

Which meant that he would have to take a risk.

Andjaba bolted upright, daring any sniper in the woods to cut him down. He stalked among his men, cursing and shouting at them, striking those who still ignored him in their urgency to waste more bullets on the hostile night. A third grenade exploded in the camp, sent shrapnel whispering around him, but Andjaba braved it, rallying his men.

*They won't believe this later,* he decided, but it made no difference. They had to get away. Nothing else mattered at the moment.

If they did not move, and soon, they wouldn't have another chance.

BOLAN WATCHED THE LEADER of the pirates rallying his men, lined up a shot to drop him, but the NSV machine gunner unleashed another roaring burst just then, his heavy slugs hacking across the trees and undergrowth where Bolan was concealed. The Executioner fell prone, as leaves and bark rained down around him, knowing that he'd missed his opportunity.

The gunner with the big gun had to go.

Bolan rolled to his left, stayed low as the machine gun tried to find him. There was no good reason to believe the shooter had him spotted, but so powerful a weapon, firing thirteen rounds per second, didn't need precision aiming. It could shatter trees and chop down shrubbery in search of targets, tearing up a field of fire where nothing larger than a mouse or creeping reptile might survive.

There were two ways to take the gunner: from a distance, with the AK-47, or by getting closer, circling around his blind side somehow, while he concentrated on the havoc he was wreaking with his NSV. Both methods had their drawbacks, with the worst scenario involving sudden death.

What else was new?

Bolan made his decision, saw potential in it if he reached the boat and boarded it without having his head blown off. The pirate craft was larger than his Zodiac, and faster, vastly better armed. If he could capture it, empty the NSV into the camp, then take the boat and flee, he thought there was a good chance that his targets would pursue him in the other two.

Or, they might take off in the opposite direction, sure.

It was a gamble, just like every other move he'd made in combat since the first time he'd seen action as a Green Beret. Audacity was half the battle, and the rest, sometimes, came down to luck.

Bolan moved out, scuttling crablike through darkness where he knew a deadly snake or scorpion might strike at any second, hoping the hellacious racket and vibrations from the battle would have sent them fleeing toward a safer hunting ground. Venom was way down on the list of Bolan's worries at the moment, while lead poisoning was at the top.

A fleeing pirate stumbled over one of Bolan's legs, then rose and ran on without looking back, perhaps thinking a tree root had upended him. The bruising impact hurt, but Bolan had no time or opportunity to walk it off. He kept on crawling, reached the river's bank, and slithered down its muddy slope into the water.

Thinking, *crocodiles*.

If they were there, none found him as he struck off toward the line of tethered speedboats, three presumably in shape to travel, while the fourth might be out of whack from his grenade blast. He passed the first boat, clinging to its gunwale with his free hand, still unnoticed, focused on the second craft in line and its machine gunner.

A few more yards....

Up close, his ears rang with the NSV's staccatto hammering, an almost deafening cacophony. The man behind the weapon obviously wouldn't hear him coming, but he ought to feel the speedboat tip as Bolan hauled himself aboard. That was the crucial moment, when it all came down to do or die.

No time to waste, as Bolan clutched the speedboat's rail and lunged out of the murky river, water streaming from him in a dark cascade. Boarding took both hands, leaving him effectively unarmed as he set foot on the deck—but The Executioner was never quite defenseless.

As the pirate turned to face him, gaping, Bolan rushed his startled enemy and lashed out with the long edge of one flattened hand. It caught the shooter's throat, cracked something vital inside there and swept him overboard.

Crouching behind the NSV, Bolan grabbed its pistol grip and swung the weapon's smoking muzzle toward his enemies.

## 2

*Windhoek Hosea Kutako International Airport:*
*One day earlier*

Bolan had entered Namibia without fanfare, traveling as Matthew Cooper. His passport was legitimate, within its limits: printed on one of the blanks Stony Man Farm secured from the State Department, correct in every way except for the false name and address listed for its holder. It would pass inspection anywhere on earth, taking the worry factor out of border crossings. After that, however, he was on his own.

Customs was easy, sliding through without inspection of his bag. The uniformed attendant didn't really seem to notice Bolan, looking past him toward the couple that was next in line. Young, Arabic and nervous-looking, they were virtually begging for a shakedown. Bolan wished them well—or not, if they were smugglers, terrorists, whatever—and moved on to claim his rental car.

The clerk was middle-age, ebony-skinned and spoke excellent English—Namibia's official language in a nation that also recognized German from colonial times, plus a half dozen regional dialects. Bolan's rental car was a Volkswagen Jetta NCS—a compact sedan, four-door, with a 170-horsepower 2.5-liter engine. The white paint job, with any luck, would pass unnoticed in the city and hold dust on rural roads to cut the polished shine. The credit card that Bolan used also identified him as Matt Cooper. It was an AmEx Platinum, no limit, billed to a Virginia mail drop where the tab was always paid on time, in full. It cleared without a hitch, and he was on his way.

The airport, named for a Herero tribal chief and early nationalist leader, was located twenty-eight miles east of Windhoek. Modernized in 2009, it had one terminal plus an arrivals and departures hall. Bolan had no problem finding his way out of the parking lot and onto Highway B6 westbound toward the capital. He kept pace with the traffic flow around him, watching out for speed signs on the way and spotting none. The good news: he saw no police, either.

Windhoek was established as an Afrikaner settlement in 1840, likely chosen for the local hot springs that led aboriginal inhabitants to call it *Otjomuise,* "place of steam." Today, those springs lie near the city's center and remain a draw for locals and tourists alike. Three hundred thousand people occupy the capital and its thirty-odd suburbs, seven percent of Namibia's overall population. Highways linking Windhoek to the cities of Gobabis, Okahandja and Rehoboth were built with desert flash-flooding in mind, but the capital's main drag—Independence Avenue, formerly *Kaiserstraße*—did not get its first coat of asphalt until 1928.

Germany had claimed Namibia—then German South-West Africa—in 1884, to forestall British incursions. When Herero and Namaqua tribesmen took up arms against the occupying army in 1904, General Lothar von Trotha had launched a three-year genocidal campaign that claimed 110,000 native lives within three years, many killed by systematic poisoning of desert wells. South Africa occupied the territory in 1915 and maintained its notorious racist standards until 1988, when independence climaxed two decades of armed rebellion by the South West Africa Peoples' Organization. Today, SWAPO is Namibia's dominant political party and a full member of the Socialist International, prone to denial of alleged human rights violations. While nominally allied with neighboring Angola, SWAPO has also granted sanctuary of a sort to Angolan rebels battling for radical change in their homeland, including independence for the small north-Angolan province of Cabinda.

And some of them were pirates, too, supporting their movement by ransoming ships and their cargoes collected at sea. Hal Brognola had briefed Bolan on the problem, stateside, before Bolan had caught a transatlantic flight from Newark Liberty International Airport to Portugal's Lisbon Portela Airport, and on from there to Windhoek. Attacks at sea included raids on U.S. merchant vessels, most recently the MV *Cassowary* with her captain and five crewmen murdered.

Piracy aside, the rebel movement also filled its coffers by importing illegal drugs from South Africa. *Dagga*—marijuana—was the drug of choice for most Namibian users, though cocaine, heroin and LSD were also making inroads, and legislative efforts to hike prison terms for drug addicts had failed in the face of widespread public opposition. That was good for the smugglers, since prohibition kept street prices inflated, and the insurrectionists who peddled drugs for profit evidently saw no conflict with their high-minded ideals.

Bolan himself had never been a blue-nosed moralist where drugs or any other substance was concerned. By most standards he was a libertarian, but he had also learned firsthand that vicious predators infested every form of traffic in forbidden goods and services. The profits gleaned from *dagga* sales loaded the weapons pirates used to hijack ships at sea, primed the explosives left by terrorists to murder innocent civilians and equipped assassins for attacks on democratically elected leaders.

He would stop that, if he could.

But first, he needed hardware.

ASSER TJIRIANGE RAN an import business in the Katutura suburb of Windhoek. According to the guidebook Bolan carried, *Katutura* translated from the Herero language as "the place where we do not want to live." Created in 1961 for resettlement of blacks uprooted from the present-day Hochland

Park sector, Katutura had overcome its stigma as a ghetto during recent years, boasting small but decent homes and the ten-thousand-seat Sam Nujoma Stadium.

Tjiriange's shop was located in Katutura Central, on a short street featuring a jeweler, two automotive garages, a fast-food restaurant and a cut-rate furniture store. Ostensibly, Tjiriange imported native art and handicrafts from Angola, Botswana and South Africa, selling them at marked-up prices to collectors in Windhoek and overseas. And while, in fact, he earned a living from that trade, it was his *other* line of work that let him buy a mini mansion in the formerly all-white enclave of Pioneer Park.

Tjiriange's other trade involved illicit arms.

NAMIBIA IS A WELL-ARMED country. Police estimate that some 260,000 firearms reside in civilian hands, though less than 98,000 are legally registered under the nation's Arms and Ammunition Act. Authorities receive an average five hundred applications for gun licenses each week, many of which are denied. The street price for an AK-47 rifle averages $250, although military-style weapons and imitations of the same cannot be purchased legally without a special license. On the other hand, no permits are required to carry pistols in public places, concealed or otherwise. But the impact of those weapons on society is difficult to judge, since Namibian authorities stopped reporting homicide statistics in 2004.

None of which meant anything to Bolan as he went shopping for hardware in Katutura. Tjiriange greeted him like a long-lost friend, alerted by a phone call to expect a special customer with ample cash in hand. He locked the shop's front door and hung a closed sign on it before leading Bolan through the aisles of wicker furniture, carved figurines and other items offered to the general public, to an office at the rear. From there, a door opened behind a rack of jackets hanging in a narrow closet, granting them admission to a second showroom, hidden from the public eye.

Bolan knew what he wanted, more or less, but looked at everything Tjiriange had for sale. In addition to the AK-47 with its GP-30 launcher and the sleek Beretta 92, he also took a Dragunov sniper rifle chambered in 7.62x54 mmR, fitted with a PSO-1 telescopic sight. Although uncertain whether he'd be making any long shots, Bolan still preferred to have an extra weapon and not need it, than to miss it in a crunch and find himself outgunned.

And, as an afterthought, he picked up half a dozen Mini MS-803 mines with radio-remote ignition switches, the South African equivalent of Claymores manufactured in the States.

He paid the tab with cash acquired before he'd left the States.

Once he left the shop, the next matter on Bolan's mind was a meeting with a target who had no idea The Executioner existed, much less that he'd flown to Namibia specifically for their impending tête-à-tête. Forewarned, the man might have tried to leave the city—or the country—and that didn't fit with Bolan's plans.

One unexpected meeting coming up.

Whether the stranger Bolan sought survived the meet or not would be entirely up to him, depending on his level of cooperation and the prospect that he'd keep his mouth shut afterward.

On second thought, his chances didn't look that good at all.

NITO CHIVUKUVUKU MISSED the nightlife in Luanda, where five million people thronged the streets, not counting foreign visitors, and anything you might imagine or desire was readily available for sale. Windhoek, one-fifth the size of the Angolan capital, had opportunities for sin, of course, but they were limited, mundane. It was like hoping for a giant, super-modern shopping mall and being stuck inside a rural village's pathetic general store.

The bottom line: Chivukuvuku wished he could go home.

The *other* bottom line: if he went home, he likely would be dead within a month.

He had worn out his welcome in Luanda and—to be

honest—throughout his homeland generally. The Angolan National Police would love to lay their hands on Chivukuvuku, and he did not relish the idea of screaming out his final breaths inside some filthy dungeon. When he went home, *if* he ever went home, it would be as a heroic liberator of his people, honored for his sacrifice on their behalf.

And yes, beloved by all the ladies, too.

But in the meantime, there was work to do in Windhoek and along the cruel coast of Namibia. So close to home, and yet so far away. Until the final day of victory, there would be guns and drugs to smuggle, ships to loot or hold for ransom, building up the MLF's war chest. And if he skimmed some off the top, who in his right mind would suggest that any soldier in the field should be denied a taste of pleasure, every now and then?

On this night, for instance.

He had started off at the Ten Bells, a pub on Werner List Street that displayed no bells, much less the ten it advertised. From there, glowing from the Starr African rum inside him, he was headed for the brothel run by Madame Charmelle Jorse on Sam Nujoma Street. The night was warm, as always, and the four-block walk would sober him enough to make sure that he chose a pretty girl and not a discount special.

Buzzed as he was, and looking forward to the climax of his evening. Chivukuvuku paid no real attention to the traffic flowing past him. He kept his distance from the curb, where a less steady man might lurch into the street and spoil his happy ending. If questioned afterward, Chivukuvuku could not honestly have said he saw the white Volkswagen pass him by and turn into a cross street one block farther south. In terms of model, year or who was at the wheel, he would have been a hopeless case.

If anyone had asked.

As it turned out, however, no one would.

When Chivukuvuku reached the corner where the Volkswagen had turned unnoticed, he was mildly startled by the vision of a white man dressed in casual attire. Mildly surprised, because he knew, on some level, that roughly one-sixth of the city's populace was white. And he saw them every so often, particularly if his dealings took him to the central business district, but he rarely met a white man on his nightly prowls.

Not quite anticipating trouble, Chivukuvuku edged a little closer to the curb, putting some extra space between the white man and himself, still conscious of the traffic passing on his left. A tight spot, viewed from one perspective, but he had survived in tighter and emerged the winner.

Besides, Chivukuvuku had a gun.

So did the white man, as he soon found out. One moment, as they stood at the corner, waiting for the light to change, there was a safe six feet between them. The next, he saw the white man moving, felt the firm touch of a gun's muzzle against his ribs.

"It's silenced," the stranger said, speaking perfect English. "You can come with me or have a fall in traffic. Time to choose."

"Who are you? What do you—"

"I'll ask the questions, somewhere else. Time's up."

"All right! I'll come with you."

A hand snaked underneath Chivukuvuku's lightweight jacket, found his gun and made it vanish.

"This way," the white man said, steering Chivukuvuku to their right, along a side street that seemed suddenly deserted. When they reached a white car and the right rear door was already opened for him, his abductor said, "Climb in and take a nap."

"A nap?" Chivukuvuku was confused, as well as frightened.

"In," the stranger said, his silenced pistol prodding.

Chivukuvuku stooped to do as he was told, felt something strike his skull behind one ear and tumbled into darkness streaked by shooting stars.

THE YOUNG ANGOLAN REBEL didn't want to die. That much was clear when he awoke, bound to a tree with duct tape, on the outskirts of a Windhoek suburb curiously called Havana.

There'd been no time for The Executioner to rent a private space, and he had not believed that there would be a need.

His business with the captive wouldn't take that long.

"I only have three questions," Bolan said. "The first—where can I find your boats?"

"What boats?" the prisoner replied. "I don't know—"

The Beretta coughed. Its bullet clipped the target's left earlobe. His mouth fell open and a cry of pain was building in his throat when Bolan plugged it with the pistol's silence.

"I don't like torture," he informed the prisoner. "I've never trusted it, and, frankly, don't have time to do it properly this evening. I'll ask again and you can live or die, okay?"

The rebel tried to nod, then settled for a grunt that Bolan took for his agreement. With the silencer removed, the young man made a gagging sound, then spat, careful to turn his face away from Bolan as he did so.

"So? The boats," Bolan said.

"They're upriver from Durissa Bay," his prisoner replied. "About a mile inland."

"How many men will I find there?"

"It varies. Twenty-five or thirty usually. Sometimes more, sometimes less."

It sounded reasonable, but Bolan had no way to verify it short of visiting the site, which he planned to do tomorrow night. First, though, there was more shopping to be done in Windhoek. Final preparations to be made.

"Last question," he informed the hostage. "Where's the MLF headquarters in Windhoek?"

"What do you want with—"

"Simple question, simple answer," Bolan warned him.

The taped-up man gave him an address in the Hakahana suburb, translated in Bolan's travel guide as *hurry up*.

And that was sound advice.

"You said three questions, eh? So, can I go now?"

"What's your name?" Bolan asked.

"Nito—"

The Beretta came down on the man's temple and tempo-

rarily silenced him. Bolan didn't want the rebel running back
to his comrades, telling tales. This way, when he was found,
likely in a few days at the earliest, it would confuse them,
maybe even bring some heat down on his fellow rebels from
police. What Bolan absolutely *didn't* need was anyone alerting
his intended targets as to where he might be going next.

Not Hakahana. Later, certainly, but not this night, and not
tomorrow.

In the morning, he would have to find the smallest water-
craft available. Something inflatable that could be packed into
the backseat of the Volkswagen, or maybe strapped atop its
roof. Failing that, he'd have to rent or buy a trailer, make himself just that much more conspicuous. His first concern was
hanging on to the advantage of surprise.

"They won't expect you," Brognola had told him, as they
walked among the graves at Arlington, with slate-gray clouds
hiding the sun. "All over Africa, the pirates are convinced that
they're untouchable."

A grave mistake.

They hadn't reckoned on the Executioner—an oversight
that could turn out to be their last.

A room was waiting for him at the Hilton Windhoek, near
the city's zoo. Matt Cooper's platinum AmEx would cover it,
and if he fell asleep with lions roaring in the neighborhood, so
be it. It would prove he was in Africa.

In Bolan's war, the names and faces changed, along with
the landscapes, but the Evil never varied. Everywhere he went,
some individual or group was hell-bent on destroying others or
coercing them into some action that repulsed them, something
that would push their so-called civilized society a little closer
to the brink of bloody anarchy. Sometimes he felt as if he were
the only plumber in a vast metropolis where every pipe not
only leaked, but threatened to explode and flood the place at
any moment. Rushing here and there with meager tools, he
fought to stem the tide, his work unrecognized by those he
saved.

And sometimes Bolan failed.

He couldn't rescue every sheep from the innumerable wolves stalking the flock on seven continents. Or scratch Antarctica and make it six; the basic problem still remained. Unless he could be everywhere at once, shadowing every man, woman and child on Earth, he couldn't do it all.

And Evil never died.

No matter how many of its foot soldiers Bolan liquidated, Evil always reared its head again, invulnerable to his bullets, his grenades, his blade.

So, what?

Spotty religious training from his childhood told Bolan that even God could not destroy Evil—or that he chose to let it run amok for reasons left mysterious. In fact, if you believed the words of "holy writ," He had *created* Evil in the first place as some kind of crazy test for humankind that never seemed to end.

Bolan didn't know if that was true. More to the point, he didn't care.

His job as a committed warrior was to face Evil where it appeared and beat it down, or die in the attempt. Another round would start tomorrow, and it could go either way.

At the moment he needed sleep.

And time to plan his moves.

**3**

*Erongo Region, Namibia, Present*

The NSV machine gun's sound was thunderous, eclipsing the rattle of Kalashnikovs and the *pop-pop* of handguns. Bolan swept the pirate camp from west to east and back again, night-vision goggles pushed up on his forehead to prevent him being blinded by the weapon's awesome muzzle-flashes. Slugs the size of fat cigar stubs, each weighing one-ninth of a pound, ripped through men, tents and anything else before them, traveling at half a mile per second.

It was devastating—but it couldn't last.

The NSV devours ammunition at a cyclic rate of eight hundred rounds per minute, and the standard belt holds only fifty rounds. Gone in four seconds, give or take. A way around that problem is the use of non-disintegrating steel belts with open links, assembled in ten-round segments using a cartridge as an interlink. While ammo belts could stretch for miles, in theory, MG barrels warp under prolonged full-auto fire, and standard ammo boxes only hold 250 belted rounds.

Which should be running out for Bolan's weapon any second.

The sudden ringing silence was a shocker. Bolan had an instant choice to make: start searching for another box of ammo without knowing where it was, or run like hell. One choice meant almost certain death; the other was a gamble with no guarantees at all.

The Executioner had always been a gambler.

While a reload for the NSV might prove elusive, Bolan knew exactly where to find the starter button for the pirate speedboat he presently occupied alone. Grabbing his AK-47 on the run, he fired a short burst at the vessel's mooring line, then dropped into the pilot's chair and gunned the engine into roaring life. He ignored the fuel gauge, since he didn't have the time nor the means to fill the gas tank, even if the needle fell on empty. Bolan had a need for speed, as some old movie put it, and it was time to split.

One second, he was sitting still; the next, his boat was lunging forward in a westerly direction. Bolan cranked the wheel to clear the craft in front of him, but still managed to graze its stern with jolting force. There was a switch to run the bilge pump somewhere on the dash in front of him, but why waste time searching for it, when he didn't plan to be afloat that long? The open sea lay approximately a mile in front of him, maybe two minutes if he kept the speedboat's throttle open all the way.

He gave a passing thought to obstacles that might undo him, but the river wasn't deep enough for sunken wrecks, and stark desert meant no fallen trees. The only hippos still surviving in Namibia were found on game reserves, well inland, and there'd been no sign of crocodiles as Bolan had hiked in from the river's mouth.

Clear sailing then, but there was more on Bolan's mind than making a clean getaway.

He wanted the remainder of the pirates on his tail.

To that end, he eased off the speedboat's throttle, waited with the engine idling, staring back toward the MLF camp. It took his shaken enemies some time to get their wits about them, check out who was still alive and fit for battle. Bolan could have reached the coast, reclaimed his Zodiac and been well under way before he heard another speedboat's engine growling on the river, but it would have meant that he had failed.

A clean sweep was the plan, and that required a chase.

The second boat was finally coming. Bolan waited for a visual through his night-vision goggles, but it wouldn't do to let them close to killing range. Not if he wanted to get through the night alive.

And that was definitely part of The Executioner's plan.

JACKSON ANDJABA SURVEYED the ruins of his camp, mouthing a string of bitter curses. All around him there was devastation, dead and dying soldiers scattered everywhere, the dazed survivors struggling to their feet since the threat had passed, checking themselves for wounds.

But he could not allow them any time for rest. The enemy who had destroyed their haven—one man—was rapidly escaping while they blundered through the compound's smoking wreckage.

Furious, Andjaba started shouting orders at the men whose bodies seemed to be intact. At least, he saw that they could stand upright and hold their weapons. What else did a fighting man require?

It was a struggle, with the sound of the escaping speedboat dwindling in his ears, but finally Andjaba got a dozen men together and divided them between the two remaining boats. He climbed into the first, positioned in the bow behind a PKP Pecheneg light machine gun, belt-fed with 7.62x54 mmR rounds. Another shouted order, and the boat nosed into open water with the second vessel growling close behind it.

The chase would come down to speed and timing. Andjaba could not say where his quarry hoped to go in the stolen speedboat, how far he meant to travel once he'd cleared the river's mouth, or even how much gasoline was in the fleeing craft's fuel tank. He checked on fuel before a raid, and would have done so in the morning, but the midnight strike had caught him unprepared.

An error that he would have to correct before the night's disaster was reported back to MLF headquarters in Windhoek. If he survived to file that grim report himself, he'd include a conclusion that would mollify his masters—the destruction of the enemy who'd ravaged them, preferably after he was grilled for information on his motives or the sponsors of his raid.

If, on the other hand, Andjaba did not live to speak with headquarters…well, then, his troubles would be over.

But he did not plan to die this night. He'd lost enough men as it was, without taking a fling at martyrdom.

The boat they sought was running without lights, of course, but Andjaba could hear its motor snarling, sending echoes back to him across the dark water. He was tempted to unleash the Pecheneg, but wasting ammunition in a fit of rage solved nothing. Worse, it might defeat his purpose when he found a target and the gun refused to fire, adding insult to injury.

A sudden difference in the sound confused Andjaba for a moment, then he realized the stolen boat had slowed—or had it *stopped*? Why would the damned fool cut the throttle, he wondered, when he knew they must be coming after him?

Perhaps the boat had stalled from careless handling, or maybe it was running out of fuel. But no, when they were almost within sight of it, Andjaba heard the motor roar again and speed away, almost as if their enemy was playing cat-and-mouse.

Madness. But it would cost him, having let them close the gap. The first glimpse of his target would be ample for the PKP to do its work, hosing the stolen boat with fourteen rounds per second. He would try to hit the engine, stop the boat and leave their adversary to be captured, but Andjaba thought the night-prowler would choose to fight it out.

Too bad.

A shot-up boat could be repaired. A corpse could be examined for whatever tell-tale clues remained to its identity. Jackson Andjaba, on the other hand, could not be resurrected if his MLF superiors ordered him shot for dereliction of his duty—as they well might, if he let the enemy escape.

A bit of caution, then, but if the bastard saw no wisdom in

surrender, death would be his choice. And Andjaba would be happy to oblige.

"Just let me see your face," he muttered to the night. "It's all I ask."

THE FIRST RATTLE OF automatic fire made Bolan duck and twist the speedboat's steering wheel, swooping from left to right and back again, in an attempt to spoil the shooter's aim. It was a risky move, since he had no clue as to the river's depth at any given point, and stranding on a sandbar or some other unseen obstacle could finish him for good.

Evasion was the key, but that meant constant forward motion, leading his pursuers toward the killing ground he had prepared for them. It all hinged on his drawing them along behind him—and not getting killed in the process.

The shooter in the lead pursuit craft was about four hundred yards behind him, well within effective range for what sounded like a 7.62 mm weapon. Then again, there was a world of difference between the range at which a given slug could wound or kill, and any shooter's realistic hope of zeroing in on a target.

The down side: with a Russian light machine gun's rate of fire, the man behind the weapon didn't have to be a legendary marksman. All he had to be was lucky. Just one round had to find its mark by accident, hurtling along at something like 860 yards per second, and the man on the receiving end was down. Forget about the Hollywood "flesh wounds" that left an action hero fit to run ten miles and take out half a dozen burly adversaries with his bare hands on arrival at his destination. That was movie magic, light years out of touch with flesh-and-blood reality.

The truth: a hit by any military bullet hurts like hell, unless it slams the target into instant shock on impact. Any torso wound can kill, unless there is an expert MASH team standing by to pull a miracle out of the hat. And any talk about a "clean" wound through a human abdomen is fantasy. Get "lucky" with a stray shot through an arm or leg, and anything beyond a graze will shatter bone, turn muscle into hamburger, and leave you bleeding out from severed arteries.

Long story short—in any shooting situation, it is best to *give,* and not *receive.*

Or, in the present case, to duck and weave like crazy, until it was payback time.

But just to keep it interesting…

Bolan kept his left hand on the speedboat's steering wheel, picked up the AK-47 with his right, and half turned in the pilot's chair to fire a burst one-handed in the general direction of the boats pursuing him. He kept it high on purpose, wasting rounds to spoil his adversary's aim without inflicting any damage on the leading shooter or his crew.

Not yet.

Their moment was approaching.

Another aimless burst from his Kalashnikov, and Bolan set the rifle down beside him once again. The LMG fire from the lead pursuit craft faltered, and he pictured crewmen ducking as the bullets rattled overhead. It was a different game entirely when the rabbit shot back at the hunters, changing up the rules. Raiders accustomed to attacking merchant ships and terrorizing unarmed crews acquired a new perspective when the bullets came their way.

Call it a learning curve, while it lasted.

With any luck at all, about another minute, maybe less.

Ahead, Bolan could see a glint of moonlight on the South Atlantic, stretching in his mind's eye all the way to Rio de Janeiro. Wishing for a brief second that he was there, relaxing on a beach at sunset with a cold drink in his hand and someone warm beside him, Bolan freed the detonator from his web belt, switched it on and started counting down the doomsday numbers in his head.

ANDJABA DUCKED, CURSING, as bullets swarmed over his head and off into the night. But for its strap around his neck, he might have lost the PKP machine gun overboard, and that only increased his rage at being forced to cringe and crawl before his men.

Not that they noticed him, as they drove for the nearest cover themselves. The pilot of Andjaba's speedboat nearly toppled from his seat, grabbing at the steering wheel to save himself, and in the process sent the boat roaring off toward a collision with the river's northern bank before he managed to correct the looping move and bring them back on course.

Seizing any chance to salvage wounded dignity, Andjaba rounded on the pilot, bellowing, "Will you hold it steady for Christ's sake! How am I supposed to stop him if you can't drive straight?"

The pilot mouthed an answer, but his words were whipped away and lost as the boat accelerated, engine revving upward from a rumble toward a howl. Andjaba was relieved, knowing the last thing that he needed at the moment was a confrontation with an overwrought subordinate.

One adversary at a time, and top priority belonged to the intruder who had left so many of his soldiers dead or dying in the river camp.

Andjaba bent back to the Pecheneg and checked its belt by touch, discovering that he had only twenty-five or thirty rounds remaining in the ammo box. Was there another on the boat? If so, could he find and retrieve it, then reload, before his target reached the open sea, less than a quarter mile away? And if the faceless raider did reach the Atlantic, which way would he turn?

Northward, 250 miles along the coastline, lay Angolan waters, possibly patrolled by gunboats of the *Marinha de Guerra*. Southward, he would have to travel twice as far before he could seek sanctuary in South Africa. No contest, either way, with two boats against one.

But what if he proceeded out to sea?

It struck Andjaba that his ignorance of their opponent might prove fatal. How had this man arrived to strike the MLF encampment? Clearly he had not walked from Angola or South Africa, nor even from Windhoek. And an air drop would have left him no means of evacuation from the battle zone. But if he'd landed from the sea, there might be reinforcements waiting for him on a larger vessel, running dark, somewhere beyond Andjaba's line of sight.

Perhaps with guns trained on the river's mouth, waiting for targets to reveal themselves.

Andjaba nearly called a halt then, but his fear of telling headquarters that he had let the raider slip away was greater than his dread of being sunk or blasted from the water, shredded into food for sharks and bottom-feeding crabs. Whatever lay in store for him beyond the breakers, he could not be proved a coward in the eyes of soldiers who relied on him for leadership—or in the view of his entirely merciless superiors.

Two hundred yards would tell the story either way. So little distance left before they reached the breakers and were suddenly at sea. Andjaba's former haven lay behind him, shattered, turned into an open grave for slaughtered comrades. All that presently remained to him was vengeance and a chance to save his damaged reputation as a leader.

What else mattered, in the world he'd chosen to inhabit?

Almost there, and up ahead, already clear, he saw the stolen speedboat turning, spewing up a foaming wake before them, as it circled back to face the onrushing pursuers. What possessed the stranger to turn back, once he had reached the open ocean, with a chance to flee?

Unless—

Andjaba tried to see the trap before it closed on him, but he was already too late. Off to his left, the river's southern bank erupted into a preview of hell on earth. Airborne, he could only hope the dark water rushing up to meet him might preserve him from the hungry flames.

Mini MS-803 mines are five inches long, three inches tall, and one and a half inches thick. Their convex polystyrene case is brown. Each mine's total weight—one kilogram, 2.2 pounds—includes one pound of PE9 plastic explosive with a PETN booster charge. Most of the remaining weight belongs to three hundred cylindrical steel fragments, each measuring one-quarter of an inch by one-third of an inch.

When the Mini MS-803 explodes, using any one of several detonating triggers, its shrapnel flies in a sixty-degree arc, with an estimated killing range of fifty to one hundred feet. At fifty, the manufacturer claims a fragment density of two per square yard. At one hundred, the spray of shrapnel sweeps a zone six feet six inches tall. Each shrapnel fragment has sufficient energy at eighty feet to penetrate a half-inch-thick pine board.

In short, an efficient mass-murder machine.

Bolan had placed his mines at ten-foot intervals, their skinny wire legs planted in the river's muddy bank. Their detonation, all at once, produced a sound that made him think of giants slamming doors in unison. Within a fraction of a second, eighteen hundred steel projectiles swept across the water, ripping into twin boats and the men on deck, filling the air with crimson spray. Perhaps the shrapnel couldn't penetrate an engine block, but with the pilots dead or wounded, one of the pursuit crafts stalled out in the middle of the river, while its partner veered off toward the northern river bank and ran aground.

The screaming started then, from those who still had vocal cords and strength enough to use them. Bolan tracked the sound, locating targets, while his speedboat idled and he found another box of belted ammunition for the NVS machine gun. Loading it, he felt no vestige of remorse. Each man aboard the two pursuit boats, like the others back in camp, had been a murderer and pirate. Somehow, the police and military forces of Namibia had managed not to notice them while they were raiding, robbing, raping, killing.

All of that was finished—at least, for these few predators.

Others were waiting for him, and the Executioner had not forgotten them.

But first things first.

When the NVS was loaded, Bolan steered his boat directly toward its stalled-out twin, adrift in midstream. One man was trying to negotiate the blood-slick forward deck, slopping along on knees and elbows, while a mournful groaning issued from the cockpit. Bolan stopped when he was twenty feet away and got behind the heavy gun, raking the crippled boat from bow to stern and back again with 12.7x108 mm slugs. It took all of a second-and-a-half to still all sound and movement on the pirate craft.

Move and repeat.

The second boat had nosed into the bank, locked tight, but still its engine had not died. The prop was churning muddy water into moonlit foam, a pirate in the cockpit fairly sobbing as he tried to back it out, to no effect. Bolan considered calling out to him, telling the wounded man he should forget about it, but he finally let the machine gun do his talking for him, ripping up the beached craft from its engine forward.

One of Bolan's tracers found the fuel tank, detonated it, and lit the river's surface with a spreading slick of gasoline. The tide of fire swept out to sea, followed the river's current to extinction, while its stationary source burned to the waterline with all aboard.

Bolan was on the move again by that time, angling the last boat toward the river's mouth and on beyond it, toward the beach where he'd concealed his Zodiac. From there, five miles due south along the coast, he'd find the inlet where his car was waiting, at the dead end of a narrow highway leading inland.

Back to Windhoek and the targets waiting for him there.

**4**

*Windhoek*

"Slow down," Oscar Boavida said. "I can't understand a word you're saying."

His caller, still excited to the point of hyperventilation, paused to bring his voice under control, and started again from the beginning. It was even worse the second time.

"The river camp has been attacked, sir," he explained. "Unless someone escaped in the confusion and has run away, I am the only one alive."

The cell phone may as well have been a scorpion in Boavida's hand. He fought an urge to fling it, terminate the call before some eavesdropper could hear the rest and use it as a basis for indictment. Did his men *still* fail to grasp that when you used a cell phone, you were basically broadcasting every word you spoke over a kind of radio? Those words, free-floating in the atmosphere, could be plucked from the air at any point between transmission and delivery, recorded, used in evidence.

But this was news, goddamn it, that he had to hear. If he had lost two dozen men, the odds were good that law enforcement or the military knew about the raid already. It stung to think that Boavida was the last to know.

"We need to speak about this privately," he told the shaken caller. "Say no more now. Come to meet me at the place. You know the one I mean?"

"I think so," his soldier said. "On the—"

"Say no more!" Boavida snapped. "We don't know who may be listening!"

That was incriminating in itself, but if compelled to answer for it later, he could always claim that he was worried about airing party business on an open line. In fact, that much was true. He simply would not say which business was involved. There was no need to mention piracy, for instance, much less homicide.

"I understand, sir. I will—"

Boavida cut the link before his caller could spill any more sensitive details. Seething at the soldier's indiscretion and the grievous loss he had reported, Boavida placed the cell phone on his desk top, slumping back into his padded swivel chair. He closed his eyes and tried to organize his furious, chaotic thoughts.

The raid his man described could not have been official, that much Boavida knew without enquiring any further. He had friends in the Namibian regime, and while they might not always have the power to prevent a raid on this or that facility, they *always* gave him warning in advance. Likewise, the army or police would not send one man by himself—if that, in fact, turned out to be the case. Both outfits loved a show with vehicles and flashing lights, aircraft if they could spare it, and men in body armor shouting till their throats ached while the television cameras rolled.

Whatever had befallen Boavida's river camp, it clearly had not been a normal operation by Namibia's Defense Force or the smaller, less well-organized Namibian Police. Even that body's Special Field Force, formed in 1995 for paramilitary missions, would not hit and run this way. They had a penchant for detaining and abusing prisoners, not simply shooting men at random and retreating into darkness.

In which case…who?

The MLF had many enemies, both in Angola and Namibia. This raid smacked of a grudge that might be personal, something outside the law, but Boavida couldn't prove that, either, since it seemed the gunman had never spoken a word amidst his killing.

What in hell was up with that?

It worried him, and Oscar Boavida did not like to worry. He had plenty of important things to occupy his mind, without the vision of some rogue fanatic hiding in the shadows, waiting to attack his people when they least expected it.

And if the man was not a rogue, was not alone, so much the worse for Boavida.

In that case, he would be forced to go out hunting for another enemy.

And crush him like a piece of garbage when he found the man.

HEADQUARTERS FOR THE Mayombe Liberation Front occupied a two-story cinder-block building on Bloekom Street, on the borderline between Windhoek's Southern Industrial District and the neighboring Suiderhof suburb. The surrounding shops and housing blocks were lower-middle-class, at best, leaning toward poor, despite their close proximity to aptly named Luxury Hill.

Bolan had swapped his digicam field uniform for urban casual, a navy T-shirt over jeans and running shoes with Velcro tabs in place of dangling laces that could trip him when being sure-footed was essential to survival. On the VW Jetta's shotgun seat, a khaki windbreaker covered the duffel bag that held his AK-47 and grenades. The loose shirt worn outside his jeans hid the Beretta tucked inside his waistband.

Watching. Waiting.

Bolan made a point of never rushing into anything if there were time and opportunity to scope a target and evaluate the best approach. That didn't always work, of course, but in the present case he had some time to spare.

Not much, but some.

The MLF made no attempt to hide in Windhoek, proud to sport a flag outside its rundown headquarters. From all appearances, the setup was on ordinary office not unlike those

operated by the ruling SWAPO party—short for the South
West Africa People's Organization, which has carried each
election since Namibia secured independence in 1990—or its
smaller rivals: the Congress of Democrats, the All People's
Party, Democratic Turnhalle Alliance or the South West
Africa National Union. MLF Central was smaller and shab-
bier, true, as befit an exiled band committed to opposing
government activities in neighboring Angola, but a passerby
would have no reason to suspect that anyone inside was a conspirator in murder, piracy or terrorism.

Not unless they knew the MLF's peculiar bloody history.

Bolan had studied up on that, via the internet, while he
was airborne over the Atlantic and while flying down from
Lisbon to Windhoek. The short version was a familiar story.
Rebels in Angola had joined forces to defeat and oust the
Portuguese during a war for independence that had raged for
fourteen years. Then, as so often happened in the grim affairs
of humankind, the native victors had almost immediately set
to fighting one another for supremacy, sparking a civil war
that bled the new republic white across a quarter century.
The main contestants, backed by smaller allied groups, had
been UNITA (the National Union for the Total Independence
of Angola) and the MPLA (People's Movement for the Liberation of Angola). During the worst of it, when one-third of
Angola's population was displaced, Russia and Cuba backed
the MPLA's cause, while the U.S. had joined Red China and
South Africa to aid UNITA. Today, the MPLA was Angola's
dominant party, claiming eighty-odd percent of the popular
vote, and the losers were predictably dissatisfied. Unused to
anything but bloodshed, they fought on—some of them from
Namibia.

Which was where Bolan came in.

In most cases, he would not be assigned to tip the scales
of any civil war in one direction or the other. While the CIA
still fought its share of proxy wars, with mixed results, The
Executioner preferred to target individuals or groups that
led an unapologetic life of crime, more often killing for their

own amusement or for profit than for any cause. He'd started out with mobsters who had crushed his family, and Bolan's war had grown from there, encompassing the terrorists, drug barons, human traffickers and other parasites who thrived on human misery.

The MLF might have a solid reason for existing in Angola, where its leaders came from, but the outfit's mission in Namibia was grabbing loot to fuel the war at home, a process that included both drug trafficking and acts of piracy against civilian targets. When they crossed the line to prey on U.S. merchant ships and pleasure craft, murdering innocents on board, the rebels had invited intervention by the Executioner.

They simply didn't know it yet.

But that was due to change.

SERGEANT JAKOVA ULENGA scanned the length of Bloekom Street through Opticron Aspheric LE 8x25 pocket binoculars, nudging the focus knob to keep the field in sharp relief. From the concealment of his beat-up Opel Corsa, parked outside a coffee shop, he had a clear view of the avenue and its MLF gathering point, two blocks down.

His vigil had been boring, nearly putting him to sleep, until the past half hour, when anxious-looking men began arriving at the party's office, glancing nervously along the street before they entered and were lost to sight. Sergeant Ulenga wished he had a listening device inside, to find out what was happening, but he had been unable to secure permission for a bug or wiretap on the office telephones.

*Too risky,* his lieutenant had said.

*No cause for eavesdropping,* his captain had decreed—as if that legal nicety had ever stopped them in the past.

The fix was in, somewhere upstairs, Ulenga had no doubt of it. There was a chance that he'd be reassigned from his surveillance of the MLF at any moment, but until he was, Ulenga meant to gather every bit of useful field intelligence that he could manage.

And do what with it?

That was the greater problem. If he witnessed MLF members in the commission of a crime, he could arrest them on the spot—or try to—but would they be prosecuted? Cases had a way of being sidetracked and forgotten in Namibia, if those accused had friends well-placed within the ruling SWAPO party. Law-enforcement officers who swam against that tide were sometimes swept away, or at the very least condemned themselves to drab careers without advancement in the ranks.

Something to think about, particularly when demotion meant a cut in the already-meager income paid to officers of the Namibian Police. Sergeant Ulenga had declined repeated opportunities to supplement his pay with graft, a choice that caused some of his fellow officers to view him with suspicion or outright contempt. It also meant that he was kept away from certain tasks—narcotics raiding, for example, where the pay-offs could be lucrative indeed. But he made do with chasing rapists, murderers and clumsy thieves who operated without the protection of a syndicate.

At least, he *had,* until he'd set his sights on the Mayombe Liberation Front.

Ulenga was aware of MLF activities outside the law, and knew that some of them were tacitly encouraged by SWAPO. He hoped that piracy and other crimes that soiled Namibia's world standing might allow him to arrest and prosecute the perpetrators, but he had not reached that point in his one-man investigation.

And perhaps he never would.

But he figured he would damn well try, and…*what was this?* Ulenga's attention quickly shifted to a white man standing on the street across from the MLF office, studying the building and its neighbors. He wondered if the man's appearance had anything to do with the procession of unhappy-looking members who had been arriving for the past half hour.

Something else he should investigate.

Ulenga watched the white man stroll along the street, so casual, as if he might be window-shopping, obviously studying the MLF building's facade in the reflection of store windows. When he turned back to his car, a Volkswagen, the stranger held a rather bulky cell phone with a stout six-inch antenna rising from one end of it.

The sergeant recognized a sat phone, even though he'd never used one personally. Who, he wondered, could this unknown man be calling that required an uplink to the far side of the world from Bloekom Street?

A puzzle. And Ulenga hated those.

The best that he could do, for the time being, was watch and wait to see what happened next. Perhaps, if members of the MLF noticed the white man virtually on their doorstep, they would come out to interrogate, assault or murder him. In which case, Sergeant Ulenga would have ample cause for an arrest.

Almost unconsciously, Ulenga let a hand dip to the Vektor SP1 pistol he wore beneath the loose tail of his shirt, confirming that it would be ready if and when he needed it.

That done, he settled back to watch. And wait.

*U.S. Department of Justice: Washington, D.C.*

THE SAT PHONE BUZZED at Hal Brognola from its cradle on the near-left corner of his desk. He closed his laptop, putting it in sleep mode while he took the call, and reached out for the handset that resembled a cell phone on steroids.

"Brognola," he said to an ear in the sky, secure in his knowledge that the sat phone was scrambled 24/7. In the unlikely event that a stranger's phone reached him by accident, any receiver not tuned in to his would relay only static and gibberish.

"Striker," the deep voice replied, from half a world away.

"How's it going?" Brognola asked.

"Going," Bolan said. "I did the river dance. Phase one complete. I'm back in town now, for phase two."

He didn't have to say *which* town. Windhoek harbored the MLF's headquarters and would also be the center of its various supporting rackets in Namibia. Three hundred thousand people, give or take, and none of them was expecting Bolan. How could they, when the man was officially dead and buried?

Few Namibians would even recognize the name, Brognola thought. Bolan had never stopped in Africa when he was taking on the Mafia, in what became a very public one-man war against the odds. He wasn't on the radar in those days, before apartheid crumbled and the great colonial powers were stripped of their African holdings.

But Windhoek was about to feel the full effect of Bolan's presence, even if its people had never learned his name or any of the pseudonyms he used to navigate his second life. There could be no escaping that reality.

"You've got it covered, I suppose," Brognola said. "But if there's anything that we can do from this end...."

"Understood," Bolan replied. "I've got a couple of angles working now. We'll see how they turn out."

"Okay," Brognola said. He had to trust the man on-site or everything went up in smoke.

Sometimes, it all went up in smoke, regardless.

And with Bolan in the mix, some fire and smoke was guaranteed.

"Later," the soldier said, and cut the link as the big Fed cradled his receiver, wishing there was something he could actually do to help, but coming up empty on ideas.

And realistically, there wasn't much that Brognola could do from where he sat, despite the reach of Stony Man Farm in Virginia. Officially, the U.S. and Namibia were cordial. Windhoek welcomed America's consular staff, the U.S. Agency for International Development, the Peace Corps, Centers for Disease Control, and had even granted office space to the U.S. Department of Defense. On the flip side, though, the same regime was tight with a couple dictators who always made the U.S. State Department's Ten Least Wanted list in any given year.

In practical terms, it meant that if and when Brognola felt inclined to offer Bolan help during his current mission, he'd have no idea which government officials could be trusted, versus those who'd lay a snare for Bolan with the information Brognola provided. That was unacceptable, a risk that the big fed was not prepared to take.

When Bolan said he had a situation covered, Brognola had learned to take him at his word. If any help was needed, something feasible, Bolan had his number memorized and programmed. Worrying about it wouldn't make him place the call—and anyway, if Bolan had to request help from Washington, the odds dictated that it likely would arrive too late.

Hands off, then. Brognola would track the action from afar, and maybe give some thought to praying that his oldest living friend came out of it alive.

Maybe.

But there was one thing Hal knew from experience. Since he'd been six years old, relying on a friend you couldn't see, someone who occupied a cloud somewhere beyond the reach of telescopes, had never done a thing to put his mind at ease.

BOLAN HAD TOUCHED BASE with Brognola as a courtesy, to keep him in the loop, without expecting any concrete help from comrades in the States. They had his back, of course, but that was all abstract and far beyond arm's length. Bolan had always been a go-to guy, and he had frequently gone to it on his own, without backup.

No sweat.

Well, he took that back. There was a world of sweat in Windhoek and Namibia at large, where only one percent of all the country's land was arable and most of what remained was desert, baking underneath a tropic sun that scorched some of the world's largest sand dunes.

Plain fact: if you weren't sweating in Namibia, most likely you were dead.

So Bolan sweated, but not from worry over walking into an MLF den with his AK-47, kicking butt and taking names. Even though word had likely filtered back to Windhoek from Durissa Bay by this time, that still left him with a fair advantage of surprise. The outfit's leader in Namibia, one Oscar

Boavida, wouldn't be expecting yet another raid so soon, and not here in the nation's capital, where he had friends in power.

Friends whose names would also grace The Executioner's hit list before he shook the Namib Desert's pale sand from his shoes.

He couldn't say how many friends, or name them individually yet, but he expected to wrap up the mission in another day or two. Three, tops. Bolan's approach to war had never been reserved or easygoing. He preferred to shake things up, force his opponent's hand, knowing that angry, frightened men were apt to make mistakes.

And it was time to start phase two.

He slipped behind the Jetta's wheel and stashed his sat phone, moved his windbreaker aside and reached into the duffel bag that held a portion of his mobile armory. The AK-47 had a folding stock that compensated for the GP-30 caseless launcher's added weight up front. He could conceal it well enough beneath the jacket, draped over his arm, and carry extra magazines in his pants pockets. While not much of a disguise, he reckoned it would get him safely to the other side of Bloekton Street.

And after that, all bets were off.

Whatever happened once he crossed the MLF's threshold, it would be sudden, bloody business with no possibility of compromise. No quarter asked or granted, either way. Bolan was not invincible, by any means, but he possessed experience and skills beyond the range of most trained warriors. There were ordinary soldiers, there were others deemed elite—and then, there was the Executioner.

Emerging from the Volkswagen, he saw an older model compact car approaching from his left, almost on a collision course. Bolan stopped short, prepared to let it pass before he crossed. Another ten or fifteen seconds made no difference. In fact, if someone came out of the blockhouse while he crossed the street, so much the better. It would clear his path inside, instead of forcing him to knock or ring a bell for entry, like a salesman going door to door.

In his case, peddling death.

The compact didn't pass him, though. Instead, he made a jerky stop in front of Bolan, blocking access to the street and the MLF rallying point on the other side. Bolan let the AK-47's muzzle poke out from beneath his jacket, angling it toward the dark face that was leaning toward him, scowling through an open window as the compact's driver spoke.

"If I were you," the stranger said, "I'd reconsider going over there. They may be waiting for you, and I'd hate to see you killed before we have a chance to talk."

## 5

It was a gamble, but he got into the car. An Opel, Bolan observed, clean inside despite its scarred and dented body. As he settled in the sagging shotgun seat, he kept his AK-47 pointed at the driver, index finger on the trigger.

They were off and rolling when he said, "We ought to introduce ourselves."

The driver took his right hand off the Opel's steering wheel and made a slow move toward the right hip pocket of his trousers, forced to lean left in the process. Bolan let his AK's muzzle prod the stranger's baggy shirt above one kidney, a reminder that he wouldn't help himself by pulling out a weapon.

"I am Jakova Ulenga," the driver said, as he palmed a wallet made of faded leather, molded to the shape of his backside. "Sergeant Ulenga, I should say, with the Namibian Police."

The badge he showed to prove it was a flat eleven-pointed star, with some kind of shield embossed at the center. Bolan guessed the metal might be brass, in need of polishing. The ID card that went along with it confirmed what he had just been told, but he could not confirm its authenticity.

Two choices, then. He could order Ulenga to stop the car and answer questions, with a little encouragement, or Bolan could play along and see what happened next. He weighed the odds in record time and took a leap of faith.

"Have you been trailing me?" he asked.

"In truth, sir, no," Ulenga said. "I had no hint of your existence until you arrived at my surveillance scene. Now, if you don't mind…?"

Bolan got the hint. "Matthew Cooper," he said. "Matt, if you prefer."

"You are on a mission, yes?" Ulenga asked. "You strike me as a man with purpose, and you came prepared." He nodded toward the AK-47 as he spoke the last four words.

Bolan sidestepped that probe and answered with a question of his own. "You have surveillance teams watching the MLF?"

Ulenga frowned, considering his answer, then replied, "I *am* the team, Matt. My superiors, unfortunately, do not see the job as high priority."

"You either miss a lot of sleep or miss a lot of leads," Bolan suggested.

"Both are true, to some extent," the sergeant granted. "I'm doing what I can. Collecting evidence."

"Of what?" Bolan asked. "Can you say?"

Another pregnant pause, before Ulenga made a choice and said, "It hardly matters, I suppose, since the Ministry of Justice has no interest in the case."

"But you stay on it."

"I am a policeman. What else can I do?"

"Go with the flow," Bolan suggested. "Make your quota somewhere else. Work on your office politics."

"Is that what you were doing, back on Bloekom Street just now?" Ulenga challenged him.

Time for another leap. "I'm not a cop," he said.

"And you are not Namibian," Ulenga said. "Nor British, by the sound of you. Not Afrikaner. How are things these days in the United States?"

"Like anywhere else you go," Bolan replied. "We have our problems."

"But you've chosen to come here and deal with one of ours?" the sergeant prodded him. "With that?" Another sharp glance toward the piece resting in Bolan's lap, still angled toward the driver's seat.

"The MLF isn't a local problem anymore," Bolan replied. "Their actions aren't restricted to Namibia or raids across the border to Angola."

"Ah. The U.S. merchant ships," Ulenga said. "I should have known."

"Where I come from, they grease the squeaky wheels," Bolan explained. "At least, the wheels with cash behind them. I don't care who gets it started, if I think the job's worth doing."

"And you've found work in Namibia," the sergeant said.

"Let's say I've got some applications out there," Bolan answered.

"You're too modest, I suspect. And I believe you're hunting pirates."

"Where? In Windhoek?" Bolan hoped he had the proper airy tone, but doubted he could sell the bluff. Not with the AK/GP-30 combo sitting in his lap.

"There was a bulletin last night," Sergeant Ulenga said. "A group of sportsmen murdered at their camp, somewhere around Durissa Bay."

"Sportsmen?"

"Hunters, I think," Ulenga said. "At least, from what I hear, they were well-armed."

"And hunting what, do you suppose?" Bolan inquired.

"I'm more concerned with who was hunting *them*," the sergeant answered.

"What's the difference, if a dirty job gets done?"

"There are procedures, as I'm sure you understand," Ulenga said. He drove another block before he added, "But they do not seem to work as well in some cases as others."

"That's true no matter where you go," Bolan replied.

"Even America?"

"I've heard it said."

"But you have Dirty Harry, eh?" Ulenga asked him, smiling.

"Only in the movies," Bolan replied.

"Too bad. I sometimes think that we could use him here," Ulenga said.

"So make a wish," Bolan said. "See what happens."

"A WISH," ULENGA SAID. "As in the story of Aladdin and his lamp?"

"I'm not a genie," the big American replied, "but I can get things done."

Ulenga steered the Opel north along Robert Mugabe Street, taking his passenger from Southern Industrial into the avenues of Luxury Hill. Some of the mansions had a slightly rundown look these days, but they were still vast worlds away from the slums of Katutura. One home here could house a dozen families from Windhoek's impoverished western suburbs, with room to spare.

"You understand that I am bound by certain rules and regulations," Ulenga said, "as in your country."

"I know the rules were laid down with the best intentions," the man replied. "Back home, the basics were decided in the eighteenth century, when people carried muzzle-loading flintlocks and the only hatchets they had were tomahawks. Rules evolve, but anywhere you go, they always lag behind the criminals."

"Of course," Ulenga said. "Because society reacts. Rarely does it anticipate."

"The nature of the beast."

"In the year that I was born," Ulenga said, "there was no internet. Russians were communists and hoarded their nuclear warheads instead of selling them abroad to the highest bidder. My country was an adjunct to South Africa, ruled by apartheid. I was fourteen years old when the Afrikaners renounced their claim to this land. So, yes, things change. But when I swore my oath—"

"To what, exactly?" Bolan asked him. "Justice? Law and order? How's that working out for you?"

"I don't claim that the system's perfect," Ulenga replied. "Far from it, in fact. The inefficiency alone could drive you mad. As for corruption…let us say that it is commonplace. You may not know it, Matt, but three out of every ten Namibians are unemployed. Half of the working population earns less than two of your American dollars per day. Fifteen percent of our adult population is HIV-positive, with an average sixteen thousand deaths from AIDS each year. Our doctors fight the plague, but there are only fifteen hundred of them in the country, one for every fourteen hundred citizens. As for the government, police, whatever—those who manage to obtain positions often manage to enrich themselves while serving others."

"You don't look that rich to me," Bolan said.

"Perhaps I am the exception that proves the rule," Ulenga said.

"An honest man?"

"Or a fool, you might say."

"Someone might," his passenger said. "Not me."

"You'd be in the minority."

"Whatever," the American replied. "I'm not a traveling evangelist. I've got nothing to sell. You have a problem in Namibia that's started to affect the world at large."

"The MLF," Ulenga said.

"Aside from piracy, they're into drug- and human-trafficking, arms-smuggling, acts of terrorism." He ran down the list. "I wouldn't be involved if it was just about Angola and Namibia, you understand. I don't fight proxy wars."

"You've said you're not political, Matt."

"Maybe I should have said, 'Depending on your point of view.' What's not political today, to some extent?" the man asked. "Religion, commerce, science, medicine—it's all wrapped up in ideology for some. From prayer to stem-cell research and the price of oil, a politician can use anything to scare up votes. That isn't me."

"What are you, then?" Ulenga asked.

"A soldier, born and raised."

"And looking for a war?"

"The wars find me," the American said. "Call it my luck, maybe my curse. It all comes out the same."

"You understand that my superiors—the Powers That Be—desire no war in Windhoek or within the borders of Namibia? They are invested in the status quo. And when I say *invested,* I refer to both their politics and their finances. Having fought for independence from the Afrikaners, with support from both the Soviets and Cubans, they are sentimentally attached to underdogs and rebels. At the same time, if support for revolution in Angola makes them wealthy, why, so much the better."

Nodding, the man beside him declared, "It's nothing that I haven't seen before. But here's the bottom line—whether they want a war or not, it's happening right now, under their noses. Every pirate raid on foreign shipping that's allowed to go unpunished is an act of war. Same thing whenever rebels cross the border. Running drugs and arms to other countries qualify along the same lines. Human trafficking brings disrepute across the board, and it accelerates the spread of AIDS. All acts of war, if someone wants to push the issue."

"Someone like yourself," Ulenga said.

"I'm just here for the MLF," he said. "And anyone who tries to cover for them."

"What are you proposing?" Ulenga asked. Up ahead, he saw the National Museum approaching on their right.

"That ought to be my question," the big American said. "Remember, *you* stopped *me.*"

And it was true. Ulenga swallowed with some difficulty, cleared his throat and said, "Perhaps there is a way that we can help each other, eh?"

"But what are we supposed to *do?*" one of the men assembled in the MLF's main office asked, his voice pitched in a whining, almost childlike tone.

"You are supposed to *be a man!*" Oscar Boavida said,

nearly shouting by the time he finished. "All of you who claim to be great freedom fighters are supposed to act like *soldiers*. Must I start all over from the first day of your training and remind you of your lessons?"

No response from any of the sullen faces ranged around his desk. Feet shuffled on the cheap linoleum that needed cleaning. Fingers fidgeted and fists were clenched. One so-called soldier off to Boavida's left muttered something but it was unintelligible.

"What was that?" their chief demanded. "Speak up if you have something to say."

Dead silence, then. Boavida's skull felt like a pressure cooker with a broken regulator. Any second, he thought, it might explode and spray the idiots before him with his seething brains. But he had no such luck.

"All right," he said at last into the silence, pointing at a short man on his right. "Stefan, you've had some time. What can you tell us of the killings at Durissa Bay?"

Stefan considered it, his eyes downcast. He had the virus, and the others kept their distance from him, as if frightened that his taint might leap between them, like an insect seeking hosts. As yet, he showed no outward signs of the disease, but Boavida understood that he had tried the shaman's "cure"— raping successive virgins by the light of a full moon—to no result. He had the smell of death about him.

"I found the man who called you," Stefan said, at last. "Hendrik Auala."

"I already know his name," Boavida said. "What else did he tell you?"

"Nothing you haven't heard before," Stefan replied. "He only saw one man. This man came from the darkness, killing. No one's bullets touched him. Hendrik thinks he may be magical. Maybe a demon."

"Demon, dog shit!" Boavida raged. "Why would a demon need machine guns and grenades?"

A listless shrug from Stefan, as if some invisible hand

raised his shoulders, then dropped them again. "I don't know, Oscar. It's what Hendrik said, not me."

"Go on, then," Boavida ordered. "Leaving out the ghosts and demons, if you please."

"There's not much more. Hendrik was shot—more of a scratch, I'd say, along the left side of his head—and claims it left him in a daze. He could not find his weapon, could not run. How much of that is true, I cannot say. He saw the man on board one of their boats, firing the big machine gun. Then, this de—this *stranger* took off in the boat. Their captain and the others who could still fight followed him in two more boats, but none of them returned. The rest, I learned by talking to police."

"Which was?"

"They found the boats and bodies. None who tried to catch this man survived. He either shot them, or they drowned after he wrecked their boats."

It was another puzzle Boavida reckoned he would never solve: pirates who fought a war at sea but never learned to swim.

"There were survivors from the camp, yes?" he inquired.

"There were," Stefan agreed. "Aside from Hendrik, three more are alive. One's in hospital at Swakopmund. He's still unconscious, and the doctors think he'll likely die. Two others, I found at the safe house outside Walvis Bay."

"And what did they say?" Boavida prodded.

"Much the same as Hendrik. One man coming from the darkness, dressed in camouflage, face painted, killing everyone."

"Not everyone," Boavida said. "*They* lived through it."

Stefan nodded, almost smiling for a second, then thought better of it and maintained his solemn air. "It's true. They both had flimsy explanations. One claims a grenade knocked him unconscious, while his friend says sand or something got into his eyes."

"And neither of them had a chance to shoot this bastard standing right in front of them?" Boavida asked.

"That's the thing," Stefan replied. "Both claim they shot him—one says that he fired a full clip from his rifle at close range—but nothing stopped this…well, this—"

"Stop! I will not hear another word about some ghost or demon shooting up the camp and murdering your friends." In fact, he didn't know if they were friends or not, and Boavida didn't care. If he could spark some kind of feeling in these flaccid drones, they might go out and do the job that was expected of them. Maybe they would act like men.

Or maybe, Boavida thought, he'd set his sights too high.

He asked, "Can any of the ones who saw this killer say if he was black or white?"

"Not with the painting on his face," Stefan replied.

"And did he speak?"

"No one heard him say anything."

"All right. We must assume that the attack was a beginning, not a solitary incident."

"Beginning of what?" one of the others asked.

"A war," Boavida said, as the pulse thumped in his ears. "What else?"

"WHEN YOU SAID HELP each other," Bolan asked Sergeant Ulenga, "what exactly did you have in mind?"

"Collaboration toward a common goal," Ulenga said.

"Which is?"

"Destruction of the MLF," Ulenga answered back, as if it should be obvious. "Or, at the very least, eliminating its ability to terrorize."

"By what means?" Bolan asked him, getting to the heart of it.

The officer behind the Opel's wheel considered that, proceeding for another block in silence. Finally, he said, "My own attempts have failed. I stay within the law and gather good intelligence, but nothing comes of it. Without support from my superiors and prosecutors at the Ministry of Justice, nothing happens. Nothing ever will. But you…"

Bolan didn't help him, couldn't force the thoughts into his

mind or words into his mouth. Ulenga had a choice to make, and once he made it, there would be no turning back. He'd have to live with his decision.

Or die trying.

"You come in with no restrictions," Ulenga said, finishing his thought. "You get results."

"But maybe not the kind you want," Bolan suggested.

"Is it worse than watching killers plot their crimes for weeks or months on end, and having nothing at the end to show for it except more bodies? I will never be allowed to prosecute the MLF," Ulenga said, "unless I catch them in the act. And even then, I think, the court would find some technicality permitting it to drop the case."

"There *is* another way," Bolan confirmed. "But if you go that route, you have to go with eyes wide open, and you can't be all half-assed about it. If you plan to start a war, know what it means before you pull the trigger."

"I don't start the war," Ulenga said. "The MLF has brought their war to me, into my homeland, killing innocents who have no interest in Angolan politics or anything related to it. They have brought disgrace upon Namibia from every decent nation in the world."

"You take it seriously, then," Bolan said.

"Should I not?" Ulenga's voice was taut, sounding offended.

"All I'm saying," Bolan answered, "is that if you join my team, there's no time-out, no substitution and the only penalty is death."

Ulenga cocked an eyebrow at him and asked, "You don't want help? Are you rejecting me?"

"I'm telling you it's all or nothing," Bolan said. "No building up a case for court. No legal niceties. Rule books go out the window, and if you get caught…"

"Prison or death," Ulenga said. "I understand, believe me."

"Look, if you have any family—"

"All gone," Ulenga interrupted him. "You know that life is cheap here, eh?"

"It's cheap no matter where you go," Bolan replied, "unless it's someone that you care about."

Ulenga's smile was bleak, verging on bitter. "There is no one left," he said.

"Another thing," Bolan said. "If you've got some kind of kamikaze fantasy, forget about it. Martyrs are no use to me, and I intend to make it out of this alive, by any means required."

"I have no death wish," Ulenga said. "But the risk…if I can truly make a difference…"

"I recommend you don't go into this believing you can change the world," Bolan replied. "It's one step at a time, and even if you win, it's never permanent. Take out one predator, there'll always be another one waiting to take his place. In fact, they're probably lined up around the block. The bottom line is that you can't kill human nature. Evil never dies."

Ulenga turned into a side street and pulled over to the curb, shifted the Opel into Neutral, turning in his seat to face Bolan directly. "If that's true," he said, "why even try at all? It would be easier to join the other side, accept the bribes and lead a peaceful life."

"The simple answer is that I'm not wired that way," Bolan replied. "Don't get me wrong on this. I'm not a saint, by any means. I'm sure as hell no one's messiah. But I never learned to look the other way or cross the street when I saw something happening and had a chance to fix it."

"But, you just said—"

"Sure, the fix is temporary," Bolan told him. "Help someone today and maybe they need help again tomorrow, when you're not around. That's life. Some people never learn from their mistakes nor find the guts to stand up for themselves. Me, I do what I can with what I've got, wherever I happen to be at the time."

"That simple?"

"Never simple," Bolan answered. "Never easy. Never clean."

Ulenga thought about it for another moment, then shifted the Opel into Drive.

"I want to help you," he told Bolan. "Here and now."

"Okay," the Executioner replied. "We'd best get started, then. We're running late."

**6**

Captain Rodrigo Acosta puffed on his fine panatela cigar, enjoying its flavor while watching his contact pace circles in front of the mahogany desk. Acosta had to keep the small Angolan happy, to a point, but he was growing weary of the melodrama that surrounded every phase of Oscar Boavida's life.

"You're wearing out my carpet, Oscar. Take a seat," Acosta said. His tone indicating that it was not an invitation, but an order.

Boavida sat, but seemed to find the chair uncomfortable. Shifting nervously, he said, "I know I shouldn't be here, but I needed your advice."

"There is, of course, the telephone," Acosta said, smiling to minimize the sting of his remark.

"I never know who may be listening," Boavida said.

"And you think they would not follow you? Would not observe you entering the Cuban embassy?"

"Oh, God! I didn't think! Suppose they know, and—"

"Never mind," Acosta interrupted, striving for a soothing tone. "You're here, now. Tell me what is troubling you."

Acosta had a fair idea already. As station chief of Cuba's *Dirección de Inteligencia* in Windhoek, he was paid to know such things and weigh their consequences for Havana. He had contacts inside the Namibia Defense Force and in Nampol— the Namibian Police—who were well-paid to forward any news that might be relevant to Cuban operations in the country. By the time that Boavida had reached the embassy, Acosta knew about the killings at Durissa Bay, had logged the body count and guessed that he would soon be hearing from the MLF's commander. He had not, however, guessed that Boavida would arrive on his doorstep without a hint of warning in advance.

The Angolan had finally worked up the nerve to tell his story. He began, "Captain, I must inform you there has been—"

"An incident," Acosta said. "Durissa Bay, correct?"

"You know already?" Boavida gaped at him.

"It is my job to know such things, *amigo*. How can I assist you if I'm ignorant?"

"So, then, you know who is responsible?" Acosta saw a gleam of hope in Boavida's rheumy eyes.

"Alas, no," he replied. "But I suspect that we can narrow down the possibilities. Who hates you, Oscar? Never mind the husbands of those women that you dally with. Who has the skill and resources to strike at you like this, destroying property, killing your men wholesale?"

"The MPLA," Boavida said at once. "They have the army and the National Police."

"A possibility, I grant you," Acosta said. "Can you think of no one else who might have cause to wish you harm?"

"You mean within Namibia?"

"Where we are sitting at this moment," Acosta said. *"Sí."*

After a moment's tense consideration, Boavida said, "Perhaps someone from the NCIS?" referring to the Namibia Central Intelligence Service, launched in 1998 with headquarters at the corner of Hugel and Orban streets in Windhoek. It was patterned on—some said supported by—the American CIA, but Acosta had his eyes and ears inside that agency, as well.

"You're getting warmer," he told Boavida. "Think a little harder."

He could almost hear the wheels turning in Boavida's head, and yet, incredibly, the MLF's top man in Windhoek seemed to draw a blank.

"Try this," Acosta said at last, when he'd grown weary of the awkward silence. "Who have you offended recently by... let us think a moment... Now I have it! Could it be hijacking ships at sea?"

"It's necessary to support the movement," Boavida said defensively. "If we got a larger contribution from your government—"

"Please focus, Oscar," Acosta said. "I am simply asking who might have a motive for retaliation. Whose vessels have you robbed or sunk most recently? Whose crewmen did your people kill before this storm of vengeance struck them down?"

"I don't recall the shipping companies," Boavida said.

"But their flags were...?"

"British and American," the MLF commander grudgingly acknowledged.

"Ah. I think we may be getting somewhere," Acosta said. "And if either of those nations was aroused to punish you, who would they send?"

"From England, possibly the SAS or SBS," Boavida said. "For America, I think the Navy SEALs or Green Berets."

"A team, in other words," Acosta said. "But if my information on the night's activities is accurate—and I believe it is—your adversary was a single man."

"That's speculation," Boavida answered quickly. "The survivors were confused, I think. Cowards, too busy hiding to make sense of what was happening. I plan to punish them severely."

"That is your concern, of course," Acosta said. "But what if they were not mistaken? What if it *was* just one man?"

Again, the blank stare from his uninvited visitor.

Acosta sighed and said, "You must have business to attend to, as do I. Oscar, I'll think about your problem and get back to you with a solution at the soonest opportunity. Meanwhile, if you have anything to tell me, use the telephone. And watch your back, eh? Someone out there does not like you very much, I think."

BOLAN AND SERGEANT ULENGA spent the morning drawing up a list of targets. After they retrieved Bolan's VW from Bloekom Street, noting a closed sign posted on the door of the MLF's branch office, they had driven to a spot Ulenga knew on Olof Palme Street, a bluff that offered them a panoramic view of Eros Park. They sat in Bolan's car, Ulenga in the shotgun seat, and stayed alert for any sign of enemies approaching.

"When we discussed the ways in which the MLF earns money," Ulenga said, "one source was omitted."

"Cuba," Bolan ventured.

"Yes. Havana first sent troops to Angola in 1975, supporting the MPLA against incursions from South Africa and Zaire. Your CIA directed those invasions, by the way."

"It's not *my* CIA," Bolan assured him.

"In any case, when the invaders were repelled, the Cubans stayed to fight UNITA in Angola's civil war. By 1983 the Soviets were helping, too. Perhaps they were behind the Cuban intervention all along. Who knows? Negotiations spanned the best part of a decade. Finally, we were told the Cubans all withdrew in 1991."

"But you don't think they're gone," Bolan observed.

Ulenga shrugged. "I couldn't say about Angola," he replied. "I'm just a lowly sergeant, after all. But I can tell you that they have not left Namibia. Their troops supported SWAPO in the war for liberation from South Africa and stayed to fight against apartheid. Now, we have the Cuban embassy, of course, and all manner of professionals around us from the friendly island. Every other year, our leaders meet with Cubans to discuss the country's economic prospects and development."

"And what about the MLF?" Bolan asked.

"We know that the Intelligence Directorate supports them. Certainly with money, possibly with arms, although Africa has no shortage of weapons."

Bolan had clashed with the Havana-based DI on several occasions, starting when it was the DGI—*Dirección General de Inteligencia*—under the wing of Moscow's KGB. These days, with communism out of favor in the Russian federation, Cuba stood alone as a Red bastion in the western hemisphere, with its closest ideological allies located on the far side of the globe. But certain allies courted by Havana in the last quarter of the twentieth century still remained friendly, happy to ignore America's ongoing embargo of all things Cuban, more than happy to buy Cuban sugar, tobacco—or guns.

"And SWAPO doesn't mind this going on?" Bolan asked.

"Some officials may," Ulenga said. "But they remember Cuba's help against South Africa. More to the point, they know the people of Namibia remember it. SWAPO has ruled the country since the grant of independence, but they're still affiliated with the Socialist International and they have to win elections. It is…what do you call it? A balancing act?"

"That's what we call it," Bolan said. Already wondering how much he could afford to tip the balance in Namibia. His goal was to disrupt a group of terrorists, not sow chaos at throughout society at large.

"Where shall we start, then?" Ulenga asked.

Bolan scanned the list of targets that the sergeant had been jotting down in his pocket notebook, pointed to the third one from the top, and said, "Right there."

*Ministry of Home Affairs, Kasino Street, Windhoek*

STEPPING FROM HIS CHAUFFEURED car outside the Cohen Building on Kasino Street in Windhoek, waiting for his bodyguard to close the door and join him on the short walk to the air-conditioned lobby, Moses Kaujeua wondered if he should request additional security. The threats that he received each week were probably no worse than any others mailed or telephoned to government officials in Namibia, but as the Second Deputy Assistant Minister for Home Affairs, Kaujeua thought a second bodyguard might raise his profile. Make him more worthy of notice—and from there, perhaps, promotion—by the Powers That Be.

In truth, Kaujeua *felt* important, and he tried to *look* important, but the sharpest suit could only do so much. Clothes made the man, supposedly, but there was clearly more to it than that. Connections, for example. And performance of the secret, dirty little tasks that came his way from time to time.

This morning was a perfect case in point. He had a meeting scheduled with Captain Fanuel Gurirab, second in command of D Department at Namibia Police headquarters. That department, also called FCID—Force Criminal Investigation Department—was the highest investigative arm of the Namibia Police, its nine subdivisions covering all manner of serious crimes in addition to Interpol liaison and operation of the country's sole forensic science laboratory. Kaujeua dealt primarily with Gurirab whenever he had special problems of a legal nature to resolve, such as the one that faced him presently.

The cursed MLF.

Kaujeua understood why certain SWAPO leaders coddled the Angolan rebels and pretended not to notice their collusion with the Cuban embassy. The party's upper ranks still harbored aging revolutionaries who had suffered much and done outlandish things to liberate their homeland from South Africa. Some had soft spots in their hearts for underdogs, people oppressed and fighting for their own place in the sun.

While others, Kaujeua knew from personal experience, were simply opportunists with their hands out for another bribe.

The MLF paid well for certain favors, using money gleaned from sponsors or from various activities that might result in prosecution of police, and prosecutors did their jobs effectively. The bribes, of course, ensured that there would be no such crusading zeal. Drugs would remain available, along with weapons and the victims who fell prey to human traffickers as slaves of one kind or another. Whether they were sweating in a godforsaken mine shaft, or servicing a foreign CEO in the honeymoon suite at a five-star hotel, each cog in the larger machine played its part.

And there was piracy, of course.

It gave Namibia a black eye in the global press and with insurance firms, but every hijacked cargo paid a dividend to someone in authority. No cash or weapons found their way back to Angola without fattening the bank accounts of government officials on the take. In that regard, the Germans and their Afrikaner offspring had taught their lowly subjects well indeed.

Kaujeua was a trifle late this morning, by design. He knew that Captain Gurirab was always prompt, and forcing him to kill time waiting emphasized Kaujeua's place in their relationship. He called the shots, and when he asked a question, answers were not optional.

Kaujeua found the FCID captain waiting in the corridor outside his office. Gurirab, for some reason, refused to sit in waiting rooms. Perhaps he felt demeaned having to deal with a secretary, or maybe he enjoyed having assorted passersby observe him in his uniform. Kaujeua greeted Gurirab without a handshake, looked behind his frown and saw a worried man.

As well he might be.

When the two of them were settled in Kaujeua's private office, the Second Deputy Assistant Minister for Home Affairs got directly to business. "Captain, can you help me understand the meaning of last night's events?" he asked.

There was no need to specify which incident he had in mind. The slaughter at Durissa Bay was foremost on the captain's mind—or should be, if he hoped to keep the job he loved so much.

"Sir, we are still investigating the occurrence," Gurirab replied.

"You must have some preliminary findings," Kaujeua prodded.

"Well…we know that nineteen men were killed. Four speedboats were recovered, all equipped for use in piracy. Beyond that…"

"Were there no survivors?"

"Two in hospital," Gurirab said. "One comatose, the other most reluctant to cooperate."

"But you have methods of persuasion, Captain, yes?"

"Of course, sir, in the proper setting. But a public hospital is not conducive to interrogation."

"I need information, not excuses!" Kaujeua snapped. "The men responsible for these events are dangerous to all of us. You understand?"

"Of course, sir."

Captain Gurirab would know he had as much to lose as anyone if bloodshed publicly exposed the links between SWAPO and the Mayombe Liberation Front. Sufficient outrage might conceivably produce a shift in government, and Gurirab had cast his lot with those who held the reins today. A change might well result in his demotion or dismissal from the force.

"I trust that you'll have answers for me when we speak again," Kaujeua said. "By telephone, let's say. At noon."

He was not asking. Captain Gurirab was wise enough to recognize an order when he heard one.

"Yes, sir. Noon."

"In that case," Kaujeua said, "we both have work to do. Dismissed!"

MAKING WAR COMES DOWN to details. Bolan was prepared, but his new ally needed some additions to his arsenal before they started hunting in Windhoek. The good news seemed to be that most members of the Namibia Police stashed arms and ammunition for emergencies, and Ulenga was no exception.

Bolan trailed the sergeant's Opel in his Jetta NCS, watching for traps along the way but feeling reasonably certain that Ulenga was sincere. If it turned out that he was wrong, Bolan would have to make a run for it. He'd made a private oath at the beginning of his lonely war that he would use no deadly force against a law-enforcement officer regardless of the circumstances or of the risk to his own life. That didn't mean he would surrender or cooperate, and he'd arranged the downfall of some dirty cops by legal means, but he would never put his crosshairs on a badge.

In this case, Bolan's judgment of Ulenga proved correct. The sergeant led him to a small house off Mahatma Gandhi Street, midway between Rhino Park Private Hospital and Windhoek Central Prison. Bolan wasn't big on omens, but the setting could have been selected as foreshadowing of the campaign he had in mind. Inside the house, Ulenga left him in the kitchen, disappeared into a bedroom at the rear and came back moments later with a heavy-looking duffel bag. The clanking it emitted as he set it on the small, square dining table gave a hint of what was stashed inside, confirmed in spades when he unzipped the bag.

The first piece that Ulenga showed to Bolan was an AKMS carbine, distinguished from its parent rifle by the downward-folding metal stock, reminiscent of a German MP-40 submachine gun from the Second World War. Next up was a surprise: a twelve-inch Steyr TMP—for Tactical Machine Pistol—that featured selective fire in 9x19 mm Parabellum bullets, feeding from a 30-round detachable box magazine. Its muzzle had been threaded for a silencer, which also lay within the duffel bag. Add loaded magazines for both guns and the pistol on Ulenga's hip, plus half a dozen Russian Zarya flash-bang stun grenades, and Bolan thought his new sidekick was good to go.

Assuming that the hardware wasn't just for show.

"You understand what happens now?" Bolan asked, as Ulenga stowed the items back inside his bag.

The sergeant nodded, grim-faced, and replied, "We take no prisoners."

"And are you up for that?" the Executioner inquired.

"I have killed men," Ulenga told him. "Two during my military service—poachers. And another after joining the police. He was a rapist and a murderer of women."

"Once we start this," Bolan said, "you can't afford to hesitate. The opposition won't. And if you come in second-best, you're dead."

"I'll just have to be better, then," Ulenga said. "Shall we begin?"

Lúcio Jamba waited for an invitation to sit down, then settled in a rigid wooden chair facing the desk where Oscar Boavida sat. Jamba was careful not to slouch and made a point of meeting Boavida's level gaze. As first lieutenant of the MLF, he was required to make a good impression, all the more so in the presence of his ultimate superior.

"What news?" Boavida asked, leaning forward with his elbows on the desktop.

"Sir," Jamba replied, "unfortunately there is none."

"Explain!"

"As you already know, sir, the police have taken custody of our survivors." Jamba did not bother with the names, since Boavida was unlikely to remember them. "We have no contact with them at the moment—or, I should say, with the one who's conscious."

"Is there no way we can reach them?" Boavida asked. "Perhaps someone disguised as an employee of the hospital?"

"Too risky, sir. If it appears that we have tried to tamper with investigation of the killings…"

"Yes, all right. But if we can't identify the man or men responsible, retaliation is impossible."

"We have the witness who is not in custody," Jamba reminded his superior.

"I've spoken to him," Boavida said, dismissively. "It's clear that he was busy saving his own skin and witnessed next to nothing. I intend to make him an example for the others."

"Very good, sir." Jamba knew that argument was fruitless when the killing mood came over Boavida. It was best, at such times, to agree with anything he said and stay out of his way. And yet, if Jamba failed to come up with results…

"I do have a suggestion, sir," he said.

"I'm listening."

"We have contacts inside the FCID," Jamba said. "With some additional incentive, they would share results of their investigation as the new leads are revealed. It's possible that we could take the suspects into custody before police do."

"Hold and question them ourselves," Boavida said.

"Yes, sir."

"Find out who they're working for and ward off any further possible embarrassment."

"Eliminate the threat entirely," Jamba said.

"And how much extra will it cost?" Boavida asked.

Jamba did the calculation in his head, adding a profit margin for himself. "Around five thousand dollars, sir. Say seven hundred and fifty, American."

Boavida frowned, then nodded. "Make the deal," he ordered. "But for extra payment, I expect a prompt and satisfactory result."

"Of course, sir," Jamba said. "We'll know what *they* know, when they have the information."

"And without delay. Stress that before the money leaves your hand, Lúcio. I'm not paying them to sit around and count the flyspecks on their wallpaper."

"No, sir. I understand."

"See that *they* do."

Jamba rose and left the office without further comment, moving swiftly and with purpose, his economy of motion calculated to impress. A phone call to the Nampol headquarters on Lazarett Street would achieve his purpose, and the bonus Boavida had approved would not be paid until Jamba's FCID connection came through with results. As for his cut, there was no reason not to pocket it at once.

Another day, another dollar, and the game went on.

But if Jamba failed to find the enemies who had attacked the river camp and left his soldiers dead, money alone would not suffice to save him. He must bring the heads of those responsible to Boavida and present them to him as a gift, together with whatever information could be wrung from them before their final dying screams.

It was a task that Jamba had performed before.

He saw no reason to expect that he would fail this time.

## 7

There are no drug plantations in Namibia. Only one percent of the country's landscape is arable, and Namibian farmers waste none of it on *dagga,* coca or opium poppies. The climate would ruin those crops if they tried, anyway, so the drugs that Namibians use and abuse are imported from neighboring countries. The heroin—or morphine base, a cheaper product that can be refined on-site—comes mainly from South Africa, a legacy of the colonial era that has yet to release its hold.

Bolan knew he couldn't break that grip entirely, but thought a couple of the fingers could be twisted out of joint, to cause the men in charge some major pain.

Beginning immediately.

The heroin refinery and cutting plant was hidden, more or less, inside a warehouse on Rieckmann Street, midway between Windhoek's Southern Industrial Area and Pioneers Park. A faded sign on one wall advertised the place as Ludik-Garoëb Storage, without specifying what was stored, by whom or why. Viewed from the street, the warehouse looked as if it had been locked up and abandoned for a decade, maybe longer, but the CCTV cameras mounted at each corner of the roof said otherwise.

The sun had set upon another day in Windhoek, while Bolan and Ulenga laid their battle plans. They had decided to begin with the refinery, a major source of income for the MLF, and hit the other side where it would matter most: their bankroll. If they took out any shooters, that was gravy on the side.

But first, the cameras.

Bolan had no idea what kind they were, whether they featured any sort of infrared technology, but no part of his plan included crashing in on adversaries who had seen him coming from a block away, with ample time to lay a trap and take him down on sight. Instead of trying to slip past the cameras and maybe blowing it, he chose to take them out.

For that, he used the Dragunov, lying well back and in the shadows as he found his first mark with the PSO-1 telescopic sight and sent a bullet on its way, the rifle's bark muffled by a suppressor and the noise of traffic passing by. One shot, one hit, and Bolan waited to discover if a guard would come to check the camera when it ceased transmission.

None appeared, and Bolan zeroed on the second camera that he could see from where he sat, Ulenga at his side. There would be others, doubtless, covering the rear of the warehouse, but Bolan didn't plan to go in that way. Having cleared the front, surveillance-wise, he meant to walk in like he owned the place.

Sergeant Ulenga's badge might help with that, if they were challenged in the process, but he wasn't counting on it. Once he'd breached the doorway that they had been watching from across the street, all bets were off. It would be war to the knife, and the knife to its hilt. Payment in blood for the accumulated debts of human predators.

The second CCTV camera imploded. Yet another wait, with no sign of a watchman to investigate. More traffic lumbered past, none of it slowing down.

"Okay, they're blind," Bolan said. "Time to go."

He stowed the Dragunov inside the Jetta, took his AK-47 in its place, and locked the car. Ulenga had his AKMS carbine, his pistol and a couple of the flashbangs, just in case. They'd talked about the use of pyrotechnics in a drug lab and agreed that it would be a last resort. While driving over to the warehouse, they had also hit an all-night pharmacy and bought a box of cheap surgical masks. Concealment wasn't part of it, but respiration was.

The last thing Bolan needed, in the middle of a firefight, was to fill his lungs with powdered heroin. One high too many when the Executioner was battling for his life.

Emerging from the roadside shadows, Bolan waited for a moving van to pass, then struck off toward his target, running hard.

SERGEANT ULENGA FELT exhilarated as he ran across the street, clutching his weapon to his chest, knowing that in another moment battle would begin. They had seen two cars drive around behind the warehouse while observing the building, another leaving, which suggested changing shifts. Drug plants were known to run around the clock, and they were always guarded, even if the lookouts were not visible to passersby.

And they were always armed.

What of it? He had made his choice, he realized, and he would live—or die—with it on this night.

Ulenga's AKMS carbine felt heavier than its actual eight pounds, and he gripped the weapon tighter to prevent his hands from trembling, but it was not fear that made his muscles shiver. In the seconds he had left to think about it, before the blood began to spill, Ulenga knew it was excitement. An anticipation that was almost gleeful, and which troubled him with its intensity.

He felt as if he had been waiting for this moment since he'd first joined Nampol, hoping for a chance to make a difference in some way other than cleaning up after traffic accidents or jailing addicts for parading their disease in public places. When Ulenga thought of all the times he'd wished that someone would unleash him to attack the criminals who shamed his homeland, it embittered him. And to find his leash cut by a white man from America, caused him to wonder if the world had tilted on its axis, turning everything he knew or thought that he had known about his life completely upside-down.

Ulenga knew he might have only minutes—seconds—left to live, but he would make them count for something.

He watched as Matt Cooper reached the front door of the Ludik-Garoëb Storage warehouse, tried the knob and glanced across his shoulder at Ulenga as it turned. His smile concealed behind the paper mask he wore. So arrogant, these bastards, the sergeant thought, believing that they were untouchable. Even the slaughter at Durissa Bay last night had failed to educate them.

One more lesson, coming up.

The big American cleared the threshold first, Ulenga on his heels, the safety off his AKMS carbine, index finger on the trigger, muzzle pointed toward the ceiling while he waited for a target to reveal itself. Ulenga half expected an alarm to sound as they pushed through the door, but nothing happened. Somewhere up ahead, around the corner of the hallway that they occupied, a sound of muffled voices drew him onward.

In another moment they were at the corner, pausing long enough for his partner to whisper, "You go high. I'm low." Then they were moving, Cooper in a crab-walking crouch, Ulenga upright with the carbine at his shoulder, sighting down its 16.34-inch barrel at a clutch of startled faces.

What he saw—the two men closest to them, automatic weapons slung over their shoulders, frozen in the middle of a conversation that had once amused them, but presently forgotten. Farther back into the room, a waist-high metal table heaped with powders, three men mixing, weighing, bagging it. Ulenga understood that some of it was heroin, the rest an additive to cut the dosage and increase their profit on the street.

The guards reacted after half a second, groping for their weapons. The big American took down the shooter on their left, stitching a line of holes across his chest that spouted blood as he fell over backward, sprawling on the floor. Ulenga shot the other in his startled face and saw a portion of his scalp lift off, like a toupée in a high wind. The dead man fell beside his comrade, and Ulenga felt nothing at all beyond relief that it was done.

They swept on past the corpses, saw the drug lab workers turn to run and Cooper was firing after them, Ulenga joining him. All three went down in crimson mist, and ringing silence settled on the lab. When no one else appeared to challenge, Ulenga let himself relax a little, but he kept the AKMS leveled at his waist.

"What now, Cooper?" he asked.

"Now," the man replied, "we send it up in smoke."

LÚCIO JAMBA LISTENED to the news with rapt attention, scowling as he pressed the cell phone tightly to his ear. That ear would ache when he was finished with the call, but Jamba was immune to pain at this moment.

"All gone?" he asked, incredulous.

"A total loss," the caller said.

"But how?"

"We know it's arson," the caller said. "I can smell the petrol stink from here. Your people burned, but it's unusual for none to get away. The autopsy, I think, will show that they were killed beforehand."

"Killed how?" Jamba asked.

Across town, his informant—Dorian Diescho, a detective with Nampol's FCID whose young wife loved expensive things—stood staring at the blackened wreckage of Ludik-Garoëb Storage, a front for the MLF's heroin pipeline. Jamba could imagine it, since he had seen fires burn and had set some of his own from time to time.

"I can't be sure without postmortems," Diescho said, "but since two of them were armed with automatic weapons, I suppose that they were shot."

Arson and murder, on top of the Durissa Bay attack. He recognized the folly of believing it was just coincidence.

"And were there any witnesses?" Jamba asked, with no realistic hope of learning anything. The neighborhood had been selected for the lack of curiosity among its residents.

"A passing driver saw the flames and called the fire department, but they didn't get a name or number. There are people at the scene, of course, but none of them admit to seeing anything."

They might have heard the shooting, Jamba thought, or maybe not. It was a district of light industry—warehouses, metal shops, auto repair garages and the like. Most would be closed at night, and those still open would produce their own racket, to the perpetual annoyance of whatever residential tenants lived nearby.

"You've earned a bonus," Jamba told Diescho. "And you'll call me first thing, with the autopsy results?"

"You know I will," Diescho said, and broke the link.

Jamba felt like cursing, but he did not have the energy, much less the time to waste. Each second counted. His first job—and the one he dreaded most—was to call Boavida and inform him of the latest disaster. Boavida might be waiting for his call, expecting word that Jamba had identified the gunman from Durissa Bay or even captured him, but this would be another blow. Boavida would not be grateful for the timely information. Rather, there was every chance that he'd blame Jamba for their new loss, thinking in his backward way that his lieutenant should have seen it coming and prevented the attack somehow.

Impossible, of course, but when his nerves were frayed there was no reasoning with Boavida. Jamba sometimes wondered how and why the man had been selected for the MLF's top post in Windhoek, but he could not ask the question without putting his own life at risk. Such was the world he lived in, rife with revolutionary passion and with paranoia that could turn a sidelong glance into a mortal threat.

Jamba looked at his cheap watch, saw that nearly two minutes had slipped away since he had spoken to Diescho, and he knew the call to Boavida could not be delayed another second. Using speed-dial, he connected to the phone at headquarters and waited through four rings until a sleepy-sounding voice responded.

"Mayombe Liberat—"

"I need to speak with him," Jamba said, cutting through it.

On the other end, the night man recognized his voice and came fully awake. "Yes, sir! At once, sir!"

Two more minutes passed before the nasal sound of Boavida's voice filled Jamba's ear. "You have news for me?" he inquired.

"News, yes. But it's not good," Jamba replied. Without drawing another breath, before Boavida could ask him anything, he launched into his tale.

THEIR SECOND TARGET was a brothel one block south of Raben Street, in Hochland Park. It was an upscale neighborhood, serene compared to what Bolan had seen of Windhoek up to this point, but evil wasn't bound by zoning laws. Wherever human beings gathered there were cravings, and suppliers of the things that people only spoke about in whispers, in the dark.

This brothel didn't have a name, as far as Bolan knew. Its prim facade appeared to be respectable enough: two-story, painted sometime in the last twelve months or so, new-looking shingles on the roof. Its porch light was an amber shade, not crimson, likely to discourage flying insects. If the traffic was unusual at night, the cars Bolan had seen so far all came with hefty price tags, some with liveried chauffeurs, and none were likely to inspire complaints to the police.

Not that it would have mattered, since Ulenga had assured him that the Nampol vice squad was forbidden to set foot upon these premises.

No problem. Bolan didn't have a warrant, and he didn't plan on taking anyone to jail. It was another case of hit the opposition where it hurts them most—and that was nearly always in the wallet.

"Ready?" Bolan asked Ulenga.

"Ready," his companion answered.

Bolan was impressed with how the sergeant had performed during their drug-lab raid. Instead of hesitating when confronted with armed opposition, as some might, he had responded instantly and taken down his targets. Afterward, Bolan had seen no evidence of second-guessing or regrets.

Another warrior stepping forth into a world of hurt.

"This time, we give the girls a pass," Bolan explained. "Take down whatever opposition shows itself and herd the johns out with the other staff."

"Then burn it," Ulenga said.

"Scorched earth," the Executioner said.

"They won't be happy with us, I can tell you."

"If they are," Bolan replied, "we're doing something wrong."

They'd brought the Volkswagen for this raid, parked it up the block and walked down four doors to their target. There were no guards on the street—they would have been incongruous, considering the neighborhood—and the pair was just in time to trail a couple of well-dressed men who'd parked a silver BMW F10 sedan in the property's double-wide driveway. The new arrivals didn't notice Bolan and Ulenga on their heels, already looking forward to a night of pleasure with no thought that it would have to be deferred.

A woman in a slinky evening gown answered the door, smiling at her expected customers, then blinking when she saw the interlopers coming up behind them. Her surprise turned into shock as Bolan and Ulenga flourished their Kalashnikovs and bulled their way inside. The latest partygoers tried to turn and leave, but found their exit route cut off.

"Stand easy," Bolan told them. "You'll be leaving soon enough."

Together with the madam, Bolan and Ulenga marched them on into the brothel's main salon, where eight or nine young women wearing next to nothing lounged on sofas and recliners, showing off their wares. They came in every color of the human rainbow, none of them appearing to be drugged or visibly abused.

Which made no difference to Bolan. Maybe the MLF's imported sex slaves occupied another site or worked the streets, leaving the high-end house to willing volunteers who served a better clientele. He didn't know and didn't care. This house was coming down, and it would take another hefty bite out of the so-called liberation army's war chest in the process.

Bolan fired a short burst toward the ceiling, taking out three-quarters of a crystal chandelier and prompting screams from several of the working girls. The gunfire served its purpose, as a husky bruiser with a pistol in his hand charged into view, emerging from some kind of waiting room to Bolan's left. The man took the second burst chest-high and tumbled back in the direction he had come from, squeezing off a wasted shot into a vase of lilies as he fell.

Ten seconds passed, then twenty, without any other guards showing up. When he was satisfied there were no others on the scene, Bolan announced, "This place is closing down for renovations, as of now. Get out, and don't look back."

"We can't go out like this!" one of the working girls complained.

"No time for you to change," Bolan replied. He nodded toward the dead man in the corner, adding, "Anyone who doesn't leave right now can stay with him."

That got them moving, with some half-dressed stragglers from the rooms upstairs. Ulenga got the madam's word that everybody was accounted for, then sent her out to join the others on the lawn.

"A fire sale, eh?" he said to Bolan, smiling.

"Everything must go," the Executioner agreed.

MOSES KAUJEUA CLEARED his throat and said, "I cannot offer any explanation at the moment."

"That is most unfortunate, my friend." Despite his amiable tone, Captain Acosta did not smile. "This moment is the time when we need explanations. If we wait until tomorrow or the next day, it may be too late."

"For what?" Kaujeua asked.

"For you, *amigo*. If this kind of thing continues…well, the likelihood increases that your ties to the Mayombe Liberation Front will be exposed."

"How so?" the Second Deputy Assistant Minister for Home Affairs inquired.

Acosta shrugged. "Who knows?" he said. "These secrets have a way of coming out when there are difficulties and police become involved."

"Police!" Kaujeua fairly sneered. "I'm not afraid of the police."

"Or of the press? Perhaps the people of your country, if they learn the truth about you?"

Bristling, Kaujeua said, "And what of you?"

The captain smiled then. "You may recall," he said, "that I have diplomatic immunity, eh? The very worst I can expect is to be sent home—which, if I may say so, would not be a punishment, considering the length of time I've spent already in your desert. As for you…"

Kaujeua was considering the possibilities. Though highly placed in SWAPO, he was not untouchable. The party's leaders would discard him in a heartbeat if they felt Kaujeua might taint them with any hint of scandal. He might even be chosen as a sacrifice to pacify the public. That could mean expulsion from the government, a loss of all the wealth he'd managed to accumulate, perhaps a stint in prison.

"All right," he told Acosta. "The police—who work for me, I should remind you—are exerting every effort to identify the individuals responsible for these attacks. We have descriptions of two men from the last incident—an African and a white man, speaking English with no European accent. Possibly the white man is American."

"American?" Acosta made a tent out of his fingers, used them to support his chin.

"A possibility," Kaujeua said. "I can't be certain."

"Still, it's something," the Cuban said. "You can check the airport, eh? Try Immigration and Passport Control."

"We don't take photographs of persons entering the country, unless they—"

"That's not important," Acosta said, interrupting him. "You'll have a record of the new arrivals, *sí?* Go back a week or so. I don't believe the man you seek would wait longer than that, before he went to work."

"Looking for an American," Kaujeua said.

"Looking for any new arrivals who were white, male, of a certain age. No need to bother with the *niños* or *viejos,* obviously. You are looking for a soldier, not a child or pensioner."

"But why?" Kaujeua asked. "Why would he come here? Why do this?"

"I hope to be there when you ask him," Acosta said. "I believe I would enjoy it very much."

## 8

Revolution is a bloody, violent business. Ditto piracy, drug smuggling, human trafficking and any other enterprise defined as a facet of organized crime. Rebels and gangsters need weapons. Where the ownership of firearms, ammunition and explosives is restricted, they must be either be imported or constructed on the spot.

The MLF, Bolan discovered, liked to have it both ways. They brought certain weapons to Namibia, while shipping others to their comrades in Angola, and sometimes selling hardware to like-minded groups in other parts of Africa. Within Namibia, they stockpiled weapons, modified civilian arms for combat purposes, and manufactured IEDs—Improvised Explosive Devices, the new-age term for homemade bombs—from various components readily available in markets, chemists' shops and hardware stores.

Bolan's third target was a combination arms cache and bomb factory, located in Windhoek's Northern Industrial District. The building was a run-down former factory, located at the border of a park where Simmentaler Street met Cullinan. Sergeant Ulenga didn't know what had been manufactured there in bygone days. In the present day, the product coming out of it was death.

Unlike the drug lab and the brothel they had raided, Bolan soon determined that the bomb plant did not operate around the clock. There was no pressing call for IEDs, no walk-in buyers off the street who needed something blown up in the next half hour. It was closed, for all intents and purposes.

Which didn't mean the MLF would leave its stash unguarded.

On their first pass, Bolan spied two lookouts sitting—maybe dozing—in a car outside the factory. They had the front door covered, but he knew there had to be a back door, and perhaps a fire escape to serve the building's second story. Once inside, they'd find no shortage of materials with which to carry off a demolition job, but that meant taking out the guards first.

A circuit of the block showed him a solitary watcher on the factory's rear loading dock. It overlooked a railroad line that might be as abandoned as the plant, for all Bolan could tell. One thing he took for granted: there would be no pickups or deliveries by train this night, before he finished up remodeling the place.

Bolan drove back around in front and parked behind a blacked-out service station that had shut down for the night, like all the other shops in the immediate vicinity. Ulenga joined him on the blacktop, checking weapons, taking in the night before they made their move.

"You know they're feeling it by now," Bolan remarked.

The sergeant nodded. Answered, "So am I."

"It's getting to you?" Bolan asked.

"The very opposite," Ulenga said. "I have surprised myself."

Bolan thought he understood, but asked the question anyway. "How's that?"

"When we began," Ulenga said, "I thought I might feel guilty. That I'd have to overcome it as we went along. Instead, I feel..." He spent a moment searching for the proper word, then found it. "I feel *free*."

And Bolan understood that, sure. But feeling free came at a cost.

They walked down to the factory, avoiding streetlights that were few and far between. Covered a block before they saw the old sedan with two men in it, facing in the opposite direction. There, as prearranged, Ulenga stepped into an alley on their left and vanished into shadow, moving out to take the watchman on the loading dock. Bolan drew his pistol and attached the slim suppressor to its threaded muzzle. Ready then, he closed in on the car, hoping he'd catch the lookouts snoozing, or at least bored to the point where they ignored their rearview mirrors.

Seconds later, Bolan stood beside the four-door, on the driver's side. He gave a little knock and when the guard saw Bolan he drew for his gun, but the big American beat him to the trigger and shot the driver once in the temple, the impact of his Parabellum mangler spraying blood and meat across the car's dashboard and windshield. Crouching then, he caught the second gunman gawping at him, reaching for a weapon at his feet when it was too late for the piece to do him any good. The second round tore through his open mouth and finished it.

Ulenga had gone silent, too, taking the Steyr TMP in preference to his Kalashnikov. No shots were audible behind the factory before the sergeant reappeared, a dark wraith crossing from the west side of the parking lot. There was no point in asking whether he had done his job. Ulenga's presence, moving under his own power, said it all.

"Place may be locked," Bolan advised him.

"We can handle that," Ulenga said.

"How are you with explosives, from your army days?" Bolan inquired.

Ulenga smiled, a flash of white teeth in the darkness, as he answered.

"Let's find out, shall we?"

OSCAR BOAVIDA GLOWERED at his second in command, resisting a sudden and powerful urge to smite the bearer of bad news. He'd had enough to last a lifetime in the past few hours, but it kept on coming, like the aftershocks of a destructive earthquake, hammering his senses, making Boavida wish that he could crawl into a hole and close it off behind him.

"When was this?" he asked Lúcio Jamba, speaking through clenched teeth.

"Just now," Jamba replied. "Well, half an hour ago, perhaps. Police have just arrived and one of them called me."

"And nothing's left?" A knot had formed in Boavida's stomach, tightening.

"Three men are dead," Jamba said, "and the factory has been destroyed. It sounds as if they used explosives from the plant itself to detonate the rest. Of course, we can't be sure until the search—"

"Is finished," Boavida interrupted him. "I understand."

It took a conscious effort to relax his balled-up fists, when Boavida felt the fingernails gouging his palms. He drew in a deep breath, tried to release some of the tension from his rigid muscles and control his spiking blood pressure.

"What matters now," he told Jamba, "is our reaction. You have soldiers on the street, as I directed?"

"Yes, sir," Jamba answered. "Everyone is mobilized, except the two in custody from the Durissa Bay attack. The trouble is—"

"We don't know where to look," Boavida said, having recognized the problem. "Our connection at the Ministry of Home Affairs—"

"Is checking passport records at the airport," Jamba verified. "If he comes up with any candidates, at least we'll have a name."

"Likely a false one," Boavida said. "And still no face to go with it."

"Still—"

"Does it seem likely to you, Lúcio, that a stranger—maybe even an American—could fly into Namibia and cause this kind of trouble for us without some kind of assistance from a native?"

"I considered it," Jamba said. "Even if it's true, that leaves *two* targets unidentified."

"Consider who might aid a terrorist against us. If you have to guess, where would we start to look for such a one?"

Jamba spoke through a frown. "Someone who hates us."

"Obviously that. But also someone with a knowledge of our operations, eh?"

"You mean—?"

"Someone who has *investigated* us," Boavida said.

"A policeman!" Jamba said.

"Or something similar. Perhaps from NDF Intelligence," Boavida suggested.

"If that's the case, how can we find him?" Jamba asked.

"Start with Nampol, since we have eyes and ears inside," Boavida said. "Your pet detective may know something, or at least have a suggestion for investigating further."

"I will ask him, certainly."

"We're looking for a malcontent," Boavida said. "Likely someone who has filed complaints with his superiors about a failure to arrest and prosecute our soldiers. Maybe even someone who has been dismissed for speaking out too freely on the subject."

"I'll start at once, sir," Jamba said.

"If we can find the foreigner's connection, we shall have him," Boavida said, surprised to feel himself relaxing at the thought of wreaking vengeance on his enemies.

"Yes, sir!"

His voice stopped Jamba in the office doorway. "Make it happen," Boavida ordered. "For your own sake, eh?"

HOCHLAND PARK, SITUATED west of Windhoek Central, once was called the city's Old Location. It was a black ghetto until 1959, when the capital's white population outgrew Windhoek Central and turned its gaze westward. The announcement of plans to uproot the Old Location's populace sparked an uprising, crushed by apartheid police who killed eleven protesters and wounded forty-four two weeks before Christmas. Black survivors were moved to Katatura, out of sight and out of mind, while newly christened Hochland Park received a nine-year makeover. Its complexion had changed again with independence, growing darker over time. These days, most of its streets are named for birds—Kingfisher, Kestrel, Albatross and so on.

Riding north on Goshawk Street with Bolan at the Jetta's wheel, Sergeant Ulenga eyed a soccer field off to their right. There was no game in progress at this hour, of course, and it was just as well. The atmosphere in Hochland Park would not be suitable for sports on this night.

The neighborhood was residential, and they had come looking for a home. It did not house a normal family, but rather served the MLF as a combination barracks and safe house for fugitive members. Police knew the address but seldom came knocking, except in the case of some crime they could not well ignore.

Ulenga and the big American planned on a wake-up call, but this part of their mission was preying on the sergeant's mind.

"What if no one's at home?" he asked, as they turned left on Sunbird Street.

"I thought about that," Bolan replied. "It's likely that the brass have got their men out on the streets by now. If everybody's gone, we'll torch the place. Let them find somewhere else to sleep."

"Scorched earth," Ulenga said.

"That's it."

"Do you get tired of this, Cooper?" he asked Stone. "All the fighting, never resting?"

"Sometimes I catch a little R and R," Bolan said, then pointed to the dashboard clock. "But hey, you only joined the team three hours ago. Don't tell me you're burned out already?"

"No, not me," Ulenga said, in spite of the fatigue he felt from tension building up between their strikes. He wasn't tired per se, at least not yet, but thought the pace would kill him if he kept at it too long. "I only wondered, after years…"

"You can get used to anything," Bolan said. And then, interrupting whatever words he may have spoken next, he said, "I see the address."

"Yes, that's it," Ulenga said.

A yellow house, whose paint had faded over time from lemon-bright to pale pastel. It stood apart from neighbors on the east and west, with strips of dead grass in between the houses. Each had a front lawn, maintained with varying degrees of care—some lush, while others had a blighted, mangy look.

"All dark," Bolan said, stating the obvious. "I'll find a way in around back."

There was an alley, made for backdoor trash removal when the neighborhood went white, still lined with garbage cans. Some of them overflowed, while others looked as if they had been used for martial arts, their sides dented and creased. They found the backside of the MLF safe house, parked there—no fence to block their access—and stepped out into the dry, warm night.

"It looks deserted," Bolan remarked, "but watch for booby traps."

Ulenga nodded, carrying his AKMS as he followed Bolan across the backyard to a door that opened into the small home's kitchen. It was locked, but yielded in a moment to the picks Bolan carried in his pocket. When the lock was beaten, the big American spent several moments more checking the doorjamb for a trip wire, but found none. At last, they stood inside the house and Bolan turned on the lights.

It smelled of sweaty men, but as predicted, there was no one home. They cleared the rooms, checked closets and confirmed that they had missed the enemy. No guns remained, although Ulenga found a partial crate of AK-47 ammunition in the smaller of two bedrooms.

"So, how shall we do it?" the sergeant inquired.

"The stove is gas," Bolan answered. "Get some of their clothes, and those newspapers from the living room, to start a fire there, in the hallway. I'll put out the pilot light."

When they departed moments later, gas was hissing from the stove's four burners, on its way to filling up the kitchen.

When it reached the threshold and the flames crackling beyond, it would become a bright and noisy night in Hochland Park.

"Too bad the place was empty," Ulenga said, as he climbed into the Volkswagen.

"Consider it a rest stop," Bolan replied. "We may not have another till we're done."

Ulenga frowned and nodded, wondering when that would be.

Or if he'd live to see the end of what he had begun.

IT HAD BEEN A LONG night for Fanuel Gurirab, with no end in sight. The city was erupting with a spate of violence unequaled in a decade, and he found himself confronted with the man who shared a heavy burden of responsibility for what was happening. A man, unfortunately, whom he could not touch thanks to protection from Gurirab's own superiors.

But he was damned if he would treat his visitor with more than casual respect.

"How may I help you?" Gurirab inquired.

Seated across his desk and leaning forward like an eager salesman, Boavida said, "I take it that you are aware of what is happening?"

Gurirab frowned and said, "Perhaps you could be more specific."

"The unwarranted attacks upon my party members!" Boavida snapped at him.

"When you say *party members,* you refer to the Mayombe Liberation Front?" Gurirab asked.

"You know I do!"

"I'm not aware that it has any status as a party in Namibia," Gurirab said.

"I mean to say—"

"In fact," the second in command of Nampol's D Department said, "your 'party members' are the prime suspects in several ongoing felony investigations."

"If that is true, why haven't you arrested them?"

"I think we both know why," Gurirab said. "Now, I repeat my question—what is it you hope that I can do for you?"

"Stop this! Stop all of it!" the MLF's commander hissed at him through gritted teeth. "My men are being killed, my property destroyed. It's your duty—"

"I understand my duty," Gurirab informed him. "Normally, it would be fighting crime. As luck would have it, though, I sometimes am constrained from the performance of that function. You're aware of that, perhaps?"

"I don't know what you mean," Boavida said, blinking at him nervously.

"That must be my mistake," Gurirab said. "In any case, let me assure you that all officers at my disposal have been mobilized during this time of crisis. They are on alert and actively investigating recent incidents of violence in Windhoek and environs. If and when the guilty parties are identified, they will be called to an accounting."

"Ah. And what if some of your own men are found to be responsible? What then?" Boavida asked.

Gurirab leaned forward, elbows planted on his desk. "That is a grave defamatory accusation," he replied. "Unless, of course, you are prepared to offer evidence?"

"I have none," Boavida answered, "but it's something to consider, yes? A foreigner arrives and knows exactly where to find my people. Does it not make sense to think that he has guidance from inside?"

"Inside Namibia, perhaps," Gurirab said. "But why Nampol?"

"Who else pays such attention to the MLF's activities?" Boavida asked.

Gurirab responded with a shrug. "I couldn't say," he answered. "It's apparent that you must have enemies. UNITA in your homeland, for example, cannot be too fond of you."

"If they're responsible for this, it is an act of war against

Namibia! Perhaps I should be speaking to the army, rather than to you?"

"I'm sure they would be thrilled to hear from you," Gurirab said.

"But it is your job to protect my people!"

"On that subject, when you say *your* people and *your* property, may I assume that you're referring to the individuals and structures damaged in the various attacks of late?"

"What else?" Boavida asked.

"So…we have a gang of pirates with illegal weapons, an apparent drug laboratory with more weapons and a house of prostitution. Are there any members of your 'party' who obey the law?"

It took a moment for the MLF commander to recover his composure. When he could control his voice, he said, "I must tell you that I resent—"

"Feel free to lodge a full complaint with my superiors," Gurirab interrupted him. "If I am fortunate, perhaps they will demote me to a post where I can once again arrest the scum of Windhoek, rather than protecting them. Meanwhile, if you'll excuse me, I am busy looking for the men who've inconvenienced you."

Gurirab watched as Boavida stormed out of his office, wondering if he had doomed his own career. And he was rather startled to discover that he didn't care.

AFTER STRIKING OUT in Hochland Park, Bolan wanted a better target for his next strike. Running down the list he had compiled with Ulenga, he picked another arms cache in the Windhoek suburb known as Rocky Crest. They took the Western Bypass south to Otjomuise Road, then traveled west again to Sando Road and followed it into the heart of Rocky Crest. No bird names there. Instead, the streets had geographic monikers: Iceland, Long Island, Falkland, Tenerife.

The place they wanted was on Gotland Road, disguised as a convenience store. While it sold groceries and smokes out front, the back room was supposed to be a storehouse for assorted arms and ammunition stockpiled by the MLF, either awaiting use inside Namibia or shipment out of the country. The arsenal was known to law enforcement, but the MLF's allies in government had placed it out of bounds for raiding.

Sadly for the rebels, those elected stooges had no influence over the Executioner.

The shop, as indicated by the splash of neon reading Day & Nite, was open twenty-four hours a day. The clerk on duty as they entered was a beefy man with deep scars on a round face framed by dreadlocks. As they entered, he was reaching underneath the counter for a weapon or a panic button, neither part of Bolan's plan.

"Stand easy," Bolan warned him, covering the night man with his silencer-equipped Beretta.

"I don't know the combination to the safe," he told them, pointing to a sign that verified that fact, thumbtacked to the nearby wall.

"No problem," Bolan said. "We're here to see your special stock in back."

The guy considered the request for two or three heartbeats, then made his move again, lunging beneath the register. Bolan's Beretta coughed and opened up a keyhole on the man's forehead, dark blood spouting from it as he went down.

The stout door to the gun room had a padlock on it, but the 92-F's Parabellum shockers rapidly detached it from the doorjamb. Seconds later, Bolan and Ulenga were inside the arsenal, surrounded by wall racks of automatic weapons, crates of ammunition and plastic explosives neatly stacked before them.

"If you see something you like," Bolan said, "put it on your shopping list."

"More ammunition would be useful," his companion noted.

"Right. Some of this plastic might be handy, too, if they have detonators," Bolan said.

They did.

Between them, Bolan and Ulenga moved their latest acquisitions to the store's front room, then Bolan doubled back to prime a Semtex charge he judged was large enough to trash the rest beyond repair. Leaving, they turned the open sign around to show the store was closed, and locked the door behind them to prevent some innocent from wandering inside before it blew.

Back in the car, Ulenga said, "I should have gotten coffee."

"Never mind," Bolan replied. "We'll find another place, my treat. We've got all night."

## 9

"Can you believe it!" Oscar Boavida raged. "I had to sit there in his office while he said that I—that *all* of us—are common criminals!"

Jamba saw no value in reminding Boavida that he had demanded an after-hours audience with Gurirab at Nampol headquarters, a risky move at best, under the present circumstances. Rather, he replied, "Not *common* criminals, perhaps."

The MLF commander rounded on him, snapping, "What is that supposed to mean?"

Jamba allowed himself a shrug. "Consider it from his view. He is a police officer. We break laws. We are, in fact, committing crimes."

"But for a higher good!"

"Of course, sir," Jamba answered, soothingly. "But a policeman's mind is narrow, eh? He sees the letter of the law, and little else. When his superiors demand that he ignore some illegitimate activity and he receives no proceeds from it, anger is predictable. And now, with all that has been happening—"

"That is another thing," Boavida said. "He as much as blamed me for the fact our men are being murdered. The gall of it! We are the victims!"

"As you always say," Jamba replied, "this is a war and we have chosen sides. A death in combat is not murder, and there are no innocents."

"Stop quoting me, for God's sake!"

"Yes, sir." Jamba bit the inside of his cheek to keep from smiling. "I apologize."

"At least I left him thinking about my idea," Boavida said.

"Which idea is that, sir?" Jamba asked.

"That a member of his own department is behind these raids, or at the very least directing others to their targets," Boavida said.

"Was he receptive, sir?"

"He will *consider* it," Boavida said, sneering. "He's so gracious. Willing to *consider* the idea, while acting as if I'd insulted his department. Think of it! They pocket bribes from anyone with cash in hand, but still pretend they're virtuous."

"Even a thief needs self-respect," Jamba said.

Boavida shot his top lieutenant a suspicious glance, as if the comment had been aimed at him specifically. And so it had, at least in part, though he could hardly take offense without making the point more obvious. Jamba was speaking of himself as well, conscious that he was guilty of repellent acts that stained his soul—if such a thing existed in reality.

Most days, he hoped that it did not.

"Tell me what you accomplished," Boavida ordered.

"Sir, the two Nampol detectives that I've cultivated will be checking personnel lists when they can, looking for officers whose recent actions have been out of character. To start, they'll look for missing men."

"Why missing?" Boavida asked.

"Because all leaves and holidays are canceled in the present crisis," Jamba said. "An officer who's not on duty must present a medical certificate that he's unfit to serve. Only a handful qualify. So, anyone without a doctor's note—"

"Is absent without leave," Boavida said, catching on. "He's run off on some errand of his own."

"Exactly, sir."

"And may be working with our enemies."

"At least a possibility," Jamba agreed.

"Good thinking." Boavida rarely offered compliments, and

even then with visible reluctance, but he seemed to mean it this time.

"Thank you, sir."

"Don't gloat! You haven't caught him yet."

"No, sir. But soon, perhaps."

"You've heard about the Gotland Road attack, I take it?" Boavida asked.

"Yes, sir. I knew Raus Simon."

"Who?"

"Our soldier who was killed," Jamba explained, tight-lipped at Boavida's ignorance and disrespect.

"Oh, yes. Of course. His sacrifice will not be overlooked."

*Liar,* Jamba thought, but he swallowed it, unspoken.

"What else have you done, besides alerting the detectives?" Boavida asked.

"As you directed, sir, all of our men are on alert, combing the city. All informants have been or will soon be contacted. Arms dealers in particular are being pressed for lists of recent buyers."

"Don't forget the whores," Boavida said.

"Sir?"

"With men this violent, this virile…well, you understand."

"I'll see to it," Jamba said, marveling once more at Boavida's thought processes.

"Then I won't keep you," Boavida said, dismissing him. "Keep me advised of any news."

Leaving the office, Jamba wondered how much more of Boavida he could tolerate—and how much more the MLF could stand. Perhaps the time was coming for a change in leadership. Under the present circumstances, he imagined that a wise man could advance himself, while laying any blame on others.

It was something to consider.

And the prospect made him smile.


"THAT'S HIM," ULENGA SAID. "In the red shirt."

Bolan watched three men walking west along Fidel Castro

Street, near Zoo Park in Windhoek Central. The guy in the middle wore red, flanked by a blue shirt on his left, green on his right. They'd left a shebeen—one of Windhoek's many unlicensed saloons—and were proceeding toward another, either drinking on the job or trolling for a contact.

"And the other two?" Bolan asked.

"Soldiers. José Dembo is the one we need," Ulenga said.

For inside information, that would be. After their string of hits around Windhoek, Bolan wanted a bigger target, something that would make the MLF's resident brass begin to panic. Rattling cages only worked if the cost could be ramped up high enough to force the opposition's hand.

"He's high enough inside to give us what we need?" Bolan inquired.

"Fifth in command," Ulenga said. "Or maybe fourth by now, with those we have eliminated."

"That should do it," Bolan said. "We'll let them check out this saloon, then take them when they leave."

All three were packing, naturally. He could see that from a distance, even with their baggy shirts and under the garish neon lights. There might be times when members of the MLF left home without their guns, but not this night. Not after all the hell Bolan had raised, all of their comrades he had slain. Each soldier had to know there was a target painted on his back, and all would have their orders to seek out the faceless enemy, to capture or destroy him.

So they'd be alert for trouble, but that didn't mean they would be quick enough to save themselves. From what he knew about the MLF, its so-called soldiers in Namibia were more accustomed to offensive action than defense, their targets normally civilians, typically unarmed. But the boot was finally on the other foot, and it had been kicking them unmercifully since Bolan had turned up at Durissa Bay.

With any luck at all, these three would never know what hit them.

Bolan parked the Jetta in an alley half a block west of the bar that José Dembo and his men had entered. Waiting could become a problem, if they stayed inside the joint too long, but Bolan let Ulenga watch the sidewalk, calculating that he would raise fewer eyebrows than a white man loitering. Once he received Ulenga's signal, Bolan could be at his side in seconds flat to greet the three commandos and extract the one he planned to keep alive.

At least, for the time being.

Ten minutes ran into fifteen, creeping toward twenty. Bolan was considering a backup plan when Ulenga flagged him from the alley's mouth, then stepped back out of sight from anybody passing on the street. Bolan moved in, the silencer-equipped Beretta in his right hand, standing ready in the shadows when his targets showed themselves, muttering some complaint about the hour and their fruitless mission.

Bolan did not call them out, gave them no chance to draw first in the great Wild West tradition. Two quick coughs from the Beretta, and before he knew it, Dembo was alone, still talking to the flankers who were sprawled on either side of him, blood spilling from their shattered skulls. The man had barely noticed their condition when a strong hand gripped his collar, spinning him around, and Bolan pressed his silencer beneath the startled gunman's chin.

"You want to live?" he asked.

His gun blocked Dembo's nod.

"Okay," the Executioner advised him, as Ulenga stepped in to disarm their prisoner. "Let's take a little ride."

DESPITE THE NATURAL REVULSION that he felt in Boavida's presence, Gurirab could not ignore the possibility that he had raised concerning possible involvement of a Nampol officer—or more than one—in the attacks that forced him to remain at Nampol Headquarters when he would rather have been home in bed.

Most officers of the Namibian Police, Gurirab still believed, had joined the force in hopes of doing good and helping others. Those who sought adventure would have pictured chasing criminals and putting them in jail, perhaps with gunplay thrown in on occasion. Doubtless, there were some bad apples who had joined Nampol specifically to take advantage of the rampant graft found in Namibia, or otherwise advance themselves as criminals. That kind of officer was found in every nation of the world, without exception. But he thought— or hoped—that they comprised a small minority. Most officers were honest when they started on the job, but found themselves worn down over the years of making do with low pay while they watched too many criminals escape whatever passed for justice in the courts.

Could that frustration spin off into vigilantism? Of course. Individual officers snapped under pressure, and organized police death squads had been documented worldwide, from Asia to Latin America. Gurirab was a reader, when he had the time, and knew that even in the great United States, where vigilante cops were staples of the movie industry, real-life police officers had tortured suspects, even joined in lynchings.

Yes, he could believe that one or more policemen was involved in the attacks made on the MLF, but if so, they were not alone.

Survivors of the brothel raid on Sam Nujoma Street described two men, one black, one white. There were no white policemen in Windhoek, or anywhere within Namibia. Under apartheid, just the opposite was true. The South West African Police had been a nearly all-white force, its handful of black constables assigned to ghetto duties and forbidden from arresting whites. Some of the racist officers who thrived under that system were dismissed in 1991, while most had chosen to resign and join the South African Police Service. What became of them under Mandela would be anybody's guess. Gurirab neither knew nor cared.

His problem at the moment lay in Windhoek—or beyond the capital, if raids resumed in other areas. The first attack had fallen at Durissa Bay, and while he did not weep for any of the pirates who were killed or wounded there, it galled Gurirab that a private individual or group of people felt they were entitled to pass judgment on the MLF or anybody else within his jurisdiction. Even leaving mayhem out of it, the raids insulted Gurirab and every other Nampol officer, suggesting that they could not do their jobs.

*Of course,* he thought disgustedly, *we can't. We don't.*

Gurirab never raised that point with his superiors, much less with his subordinates who might run off and carry tales behind his back. His thoughts were private, and he kept them to himself. It was a matter of self-preservation, not to mention his advancement through the Nampol ranks.

But if a rogue policeman was involved in the Windhoek attacks, Gurirab had to find the man and stop him. Maybe even save the renegade before he was identified by other means and jailed—or gunned down on the street. If he found more than one involved, the task would be more difficult, but might not be impossible.

Names first. Boavida had proposed the single best approach, damn him. With every member of the force called out to work around the clock until the raiders were identified, an officer found missing from his post and out of touch with headquarters would be Gurirab's prime suspect. Which meant he had to check on thirteen thousand officers, but Gurirab could narrow that for the moment by ruling out females and focusing on men posted in Windhoek. Any officer who could not be accounted for was suspect, more so if he had been missing on the night of the Durissa Bay attack.

It was a place to start.

All Gurirab had to do was run his search without involving or alerting anybody else from Nampol headquarters. He had no more time to waste.

ULENGA HAD SUGGESTED a location for the captive's grilling. But he presently wondered whether he'd be damned for doing so. And even as the thought took form, he knew it came too late.

The hideout was a small house near the Goreangob Reservoir, northwest of town. On rare occasions, Nampol used it for protected witnesses or as the big American prepared to use it,

for an interrogation best removed from prying eyes at headquarters. Squatters had found the place on several occasions
and were dealt with harshly, but the space was empty when
Bolan and Ulenga arrived with José Dembo.

The accoutrements of inquisition were already on the premises. A wooden chair with legs set far enough apart that it was
difficult to rock or overturn. Enough duct tape to bind a dozen
mummies. An assortment of completely mundane tools that
only took on morbid connotation if you looked too closely at
their stains. A hand-crank generator trailing cables with a pair
of tarnished alligator clips attached.

Dembo took in the scene and might have bolted, but Bolan's pistol settled him. He offered no objection when Bolan
ordered him to sit down on the wooden chair. In fact, Ulenga
thought their captive was relieved that no one ordered him to
strip. If he was left with clothing, how bad could the grilling
be?

Ulenga didn't want to think about that yet.

Bolan handed him a roll of duct tape and Ulenga went to
work. He started off at Dembo's ankles, fastening each to a leg
of the chair and working upward from there to the knees while
Bolan covered Dembo. Next, his arms, beginning at the wrist,
securing each in turn to the chair's wooden arms. The final
step was wrapping Dembo's upper body until he was pinned,
immobile, to the chair's back. When Ulenga finished, Dembo
had free movement of his head and fingers, but he could not
move his torso, and his feet could not find purchase on the
floor to rock the chair in which he sat.

So far, the prisoner had not risked speaking. When he could
no longer move, however, Dembo found his voice. "Why have
you brought me here?" he asked.

Bolan answered with a question of his own. "Isn't it obvious? We need some information."

"Then you're wasting time," Dembo replied. "I am not an
informer."

The warrior moved closer to the chair. He said, "You saw

what happened to your two friends, back in town. Are you anxious to join them?"

"I'm a soldier," Dembo answered. "We accept the possibility of death."

"I'm wondering what kind of long-term health-care plan the MLF provides," Bolan said.

Their captive looked confused. Confirmed it when he said, "I don't know what you mean."

Bolan shrugged. "You're not afraid to die. Okay. Suppose we send you back minus your arms and legs. Who feeds you then? Who takes care of your hygiene? Who buys the prosthetics? Have you got a good insurance plan through the Mayombe Liberation Front?"

Dembo tried to ignore him, and was doing fairly well until Bolan found a blowtorch and a small electric chain saw sitting in a corner, brought them back and laid them on the floor at Dembo's feet.

"I've never cared for torture," Bolan announced. "It's messy and it doesn't always get results. Still, when the time's short and an answer's needed right away, I make allowances."

"Do what you must," Dembo replied. "I'm not afraid."

Ulenga heard the tremor in his voice and thought, *liar*.

"Okay, then." Bolan plugged in the chain saw, using an extension cord. Came back and revved it up, filling the small house with its high-pitched buzzing sound. "Let's trim those toenails for a start," he said.

THEIR PRISONER BROKE DOWN before the chain saw finished gnawing through the square toe of his boot, squealing for mercy. Bolan left it idling where Dembo could see it as he said, "Give me a reason not to go ahead."

"What is it that you want to know?" Dembo replied, eyes wide, sweat beaded on his forehead.

"Hit the high points," Bolan told him. "Traffic you're expecting, operations in the works right now. Something that's worth your life."

It looked as if the man taped to the chair might have a

stroke, panic spiking his blood pressure into the stratosphere while he wracked his brain, but then he hit on something and produced a kind of twisted smile.

"An arms shipment!" he blurted out. "It's coming in tomorrow—wait, I mean tonight—out of Angola, over the Kunene River. Three truckloads of rifles and machine guns, ammunition, RPGs. We should have canceled it, but Oscar chose to go ahead as planned."

"That's Oscar Boavida?" Bolan asked him.

Dembo nodded jerkily. "Unless he's changed his mind since yesterday at lunch, when we discussed it, they'll be coming in at midnight."

That left Bolan with the best part of a day to kill. "What else?" he asked the prisoner.

"No other shipments for a week or more," Dembo said. "If you want details on those…"

"No, thanks," Bolan replied. "You know the names of MLF contacts inside the government?"

"A few," the sweating captive said. "With the police—"

"Besides Nampol," Bolan said, cutting in. He didn't need the names of any crooked cops, since he was pledged to let them live.

"Um…well…there's Moses Kaujeua at the Ministry of Home Affairs," Dembo said.

Bolan heard Ulenga hiss at that and turned to face him. "Somebody you know?" he asked.

"The Second Deputy Assistant Minister," Ulenga said. "I've never met him, but he's well-known in Namibia, of course."

"And you can find him, if we need to?"

"Probably. He will be guarded," Ulenga said.

"Not a problem." Turning back to Dembo, Bolan asked him, "Anybody else?"

Dembo named one member of Namibia's National Council and three from the National Assembly, plus a friendly judge in Windhoek. Each name seemed to strike Ulenga like a slap across the face, his shoulders hunching in anticipation of another blow.

"This comes as news to you," Bolan said.

His companion nodded. "Bitter news," Ulenga answered.

Bolan checked his watch. A midnight ambush on the country's northern border left them twenty hours and change before they had to be in place and ready for the weapons convoy. Four hundred miles to travel, more or less, and that left...what? Call it twelve hours to raise hell in Windhoek before setting off across the desert for their rendezvous.

But first, he had to break the bad news to their prisoner.

"All right," Bolan told José Dembo. "That should do it."

"You need nothing more?" Dembo seemed startled, then confused. "I'm free to go?"

"Sorry," Bolan replied. "It doesn't work that way."

He saw the panic coming back in Dembo's eyes. "What do you mean? You said—"

"I know," the Executioner cut through his babble. "But we can't afford to let you go. You'd run straight back to headquarters and tip them. Anybody would. I'd do the same myself."

"But, no! I swear it on my children's lives!"

"He isn't married," Ulenga said, leaden-voiced.

"No harm in trying, though," Bolan said.

"Wait! I—"

One hit from the butt of the pistol snapped Dembo's head back. By the time the man came to and was found, it would be too late. Bolan's mission would already be complete—or at least nearly so.

"You still on board?" he asked Ulenga.

"Yes," the sergeant said. "It seems we have much work to do."

**10**

"Two more dead, and José missing?" Oscar Boavida's tone suggested that he could not grasp the latest news.

"Yes, sir," Lúcio Jamba said.

"In Windhoek Central?"

"On a public street," Jamba said. "Still, there were no witnesses, but I've confirmed it with Nampol."

"And who was killed?"

Jamba doubted that his superior would recognize the names, but he replied, "António Lourenço and Pitra Savimbi."

"They were good men?" Boavida asked.

"Not good enough, apparently," Jamba said.

"Is there any hope that José managed to escape the trap?"

Jamba pretended to consider it, then shook his head. "He would have called by now. The shooting happened more than an hour ago."

Boavida squinted at him. "Why am I just learning of it?" he demanded.

"Sir, it's only been ten minutes since I heard from the police," Jamba explained, his temper simmering. "I had to check the facts and check the hospital. Also, the doctor that we use."

"I need to hear these things immediately!" Boavida said, as if he had not answered.

"Certainly. I understand, sir," Jamba said, fuming.

"We take it, then, that José has been captured by our enemies?"

"I see no other possible interpretation," Jamba said. "If he was simply killed, he should have been found with the others."

"And why would he be taken? For interrogation?"

Jamba had to shrug at that. "There has been no demand for ransom," he replied. "If they were after money—whoever *they* are—we would have heard from them by now. One raid or two, perhaps, to make a point, before they called to set the terms."

"José's a good man. Strong," Boavida said. "He won't tell them anything."

"Let's hope not," Jamba said. He knew that any man could break, if his tormentors find the weak spot he conceals and use the proper tools to crack it.

"But you think he might?" Boavida asked, anxious.

Jamba was moved to wonder once again how this man had achieved his present rank in the Mayombe Liberation Front. Blackmail of their superiors, perhaps? It would have been much easier to kill him than promote him, but the harm was done.

Which did not mean that it could never be corrected.

Jamba shrugged in answer to the question and said, "We can't predict what anyone may do or say, if they are tortured."

"Damn it! What could he tell them?"

"What have *you* told *him,* sir?" Jamba asked.

After another moment, Boavida's shoulders slumped. "He knows about the shipment, Lúcio."

"I will call them," Jamba said. "Either divert the shipment or delay it."

"That's impossible," Boavida said. "That whole section of the desert is a dead zone for cell phones, and the convoys travel in radio silence."

"So, we simply let them drive into a trap?" Jamba asked.

"If a trap exists, the only way to help them is with reinforcements," Boavida answered. "You must lead them, Lúcio. Handpick a team and take them to the border. Meet the convoy and make sure it crosses safely."

Jamba felt the noose closing around him, but he had no

option to refuse the order. At the very least, he would appear to be a coward, at the worst, an outright traitor.

"Yes, sir. As you wish," he said. "How many soldiers can we spare from Windhoek?"

"Nine should already be coming with the lorries," Boavida said. "Take six, besides yourself. That ought to be enough for two opponents, if they even try to stop the caravan."

Jamba remembered what had happened to the *twenty* soldiers at Durissa Bay, but once again, he knew that there was nothing to be gained by arguing. Once Boavida settled on a plan, it was as good as carved in stone.

*Perhaps we won't meet anyone,* Jamba thought. The convoy might come through without a hitch—or, if it was attacked, he might be able to destroy their adversaries and return to Windhoek as a hero.

Either way, Jamba decided, if he lived to see another sunrise, there would have to be some changes made.

SERGEANT ULENGA TRACED a blue line on the map he'd spread between himself and Bolan, saying, "This is the Kunene River. It flows south from the Angolan highlands to this point, then turns west toward the sea. This portion marks the borderline between Angola and Namibia."

"Bridges?" Bolan asked.

"They are not required for full-size lorries, or for smaller vehicles with four-wheel drive and snorkels on their engines," Ulenga said. "Others must go east to Mahenene or beyond and find a dry place."

"That's a hundred miles of riverfront or more," Bolan said. "How are we supposed to find the spot where they'll be crossing?"

"There is only one road south to the Kunene from Cahama," the policeman told him. "They will use it to avoid a breakdown in the desert."

"So, they'll have to deal with border guards," Bolan observed.

"Unlikely," Ulenga said. "The nearest border checkpoint

is at Oshikango, opposite Ngiva on Angola's side. The guards are lazy and do not patrol the border without some complaint to motivate them."

"It's wide open, then?"

"For all intents and purposes," Ulenga said. "With no ferry or bus lines to Angola, they pretend the border is secure. In fact, it's like a sieve, but smuggling is a boon to the economy on both sides, so why make an issue of it?"

"Suits me," Bolan said, hoping that this would not be the rare occasion when a stray patrol passed by on one side of the border or the other. Cops on-site would force him to abort the ambush, and it would have been a long drive north for nothing.

"If we have a difficulty," Ulenga said, "it may come from Windhoek. The police will certainly have found Dembo's companions by this time. As soon as they're identified, word will be passed to Oscar Boavida. When José is unaccounted for, the MLF may worry over what he knows and might have told about their plans."

"You're thinking they'll send someone north to head us off," Bolan said.

"Likely, if they think about the weapons shipment," Ulenga said. "Or they'll try to cancel the delivery."

"Sounds like we need to keep them hopping in the meantime," Bolan said. "Touch base a few more times, before we head up north."

"It might work," Ulenga said, sounding less than totally convinced.

"If nothing else," Bolan said, "we can thin the ranks some more. Leave them with fewer soldiers for a border expedition."

"It's a good thing that we got the extra ammunition," his companion said.

"There's no such thing as too much ammo," Bolan readily agreed.

"We still have several targets on the list in Windhoek," Ulenga said. "Two or three of them are fairly close together. If they don't anticipate our movements, we can hit them on our way out."

"Works for me," Bolan agreed. "This one on Prum Street takes us to the B1 highway and the second spot on New Castle, then it's a straight run north. A call before we leave might shake things up and keep them guessing."

"You would telephone the MLF?" Ulenga asked.

"A little agitation with some misdirection," Bolan said. "It's worked for me before."

"What would you say?"

"I play these kinds of things by ear," Bolan replied. "Ideally, I can get the top man wondering about his aides, looking for traitors where they don't exist. The more time he spends looking over his shoulder, the better for us."

"How will you prevent the call from being traced?" Ulenga asked.

"I won't be on that long," Bolan said, "and they have to be set to run a triangulation. By the time they think of it, we'll be long gone."

Ulenga seemed about to ask another question, settled for a shrug instead, and said, "We should get started, then, before they send more soldiers north."

"Sounds good," Bolan replied. "Next target coming up."

THE TRILLING CELL PHONE startled Boavida with a glass of rum raised halfway to his mouth. He stopped and frowned, considering who might be calling him, counting the individuals who knew his private number. When he thought of José Dembo, Boavida nearly dropped his glass, scooped up the phone and answered it.

"Hello?" He'd nearly said "José?" but caught himself in time to dodge embarrassment if it was someone else.

And so it was.

"José can't talk right now," a stranger's voice replied. "He's tied up at the moment."

"Who is this?" Boavida asked, hating the shiver in his voice.

"You can't guess?" the caller asked.

Boavida thought he sounded white, not European, and it clicked. "Why are you doing this?" he asked.

"Here's a better question," the stranger said, dodging Boavida's. "Who in Windhoek wants you gone, but wouldn't care to have a trial where you could tell your side of things? I'll bet somebody comes to mind."

In fact, the MLF commander could not think of all his living enemies while standing with the cell phone pressed against his ear, discussing life and death with someone he had never met. The same man who had killed three dozen of his men so far, and cost him several hundred thousand dollars worth of property.

"I don't have time for guessing games," Boavida said, feeling foolish. "If you want to tell me something, spit it out!"

"Okay, two things," the unknown caller said. "First, that gambling spot on Prum Street that you forgot to register just went out of business. If you hurry, maybe you can help the fire brigade."

"Goddamn you!"

"The second thing," his tormentor pressed on. "That dive you run on New Castle—the Cheetah Club—should be collapsing right about...now."

As punctuation to the caller's comment, Boavida heard the sound of an explosion relayed through his cell phone from a distance.

"There it goes," the stranger said. "Closed for remodeling."

"Just tell me why you're doing this!" Boavida snapped.

"I *did* tell you," the caller answered. "Someone wants you out, humiliated and disgraced. Not dead, or you'd be in a box by now. Maybe this person hopes you'll run and leave a mess behind for someone else to clean up and put right. Maybe he hopes you'll stand and fight, which means you *will* die, guaranteed. I don't inquire about a client's motive when I take a job."

"You are a mercenary?" Boavida asked.

"I always thought *soldier of fortune* had a nicer ring. Whatever," the caller said, "I'm just tipping you because the sooner you wise up and leave, the quicker I can cash in and get out of here. Leave now, some of your men may live to work for your replacement. What's the difference? You've likely got some money put away for—"

"I'm not leaving!" Boavida thundered. "I'm not going anywhere!"

"Your call," the stranger said. "More work for me, of course…unless you get it in the back before we meet."

"What do—"

The line went dead, a *click,* then nothing. Boavida fought an urge to hurl his phone across the room, taking a deep breath to relax himself as he replaced it on his desk.

The deep breath didn't help.

A stranger calls his private line to say that he's been hired by someone close to Boavida, someone seeking to embarrass and depose him without killing him outright. The reason? Boavida knew that if his efforts in Namibia produced great losses and humiliation for the MLF, his own superiors might have him killed—but if that was their aim, why not simply be done with it?

Who else was close to him, and still might wish him harm? Not Dembo, who was likely dead. Which, in Boavida's mind, only left Lúcio Jamba.

*Ridiculous!* They had been friends for years, advancing through the ranks together—although Jamba, granted, had always lagged a bit behind. Had Boavida's personal success embittered his lieutenant? Could it be that Jamba plotted to depose him?

Boavida stopped that train of thought, deciding that he must confirm the caller's other statements first, before he gave free rein to paranoia. Step one was to call the manager of his shebeen on New Castle and verify a blast at that location. Next, the gambling club on Prum Street. If he found that both facilities had been destroyed, it meant the call had been no sick joke to unnerve him. In that case, the men around him would require more scrutiny.

But he'd sent Jamba out of town.

No matter. If he turned up any evidence of the man's betrayal, Boavida could surprise him with it when he got back to Windhoek.

The last surprise of Jamba's life, perhaps.

THE DRIVE NORTH WAS A long one, and the B1 highway barely qualified as such by any normal standard. Although it was the country's most important artery of travel, bisecting Namibia from south to north, the B1 was still only two lanes wide, and maintenance left much to be desired. It ran from Noordoewer on the South African border to Oshikango on the border with Angola, but Ulenga knew they would be leaving it before they reached that terminus, after they'd passed through Okahandja, Otjiwarongo, Otavi, Tsumeb and Ondangwa.

Once they left the B1 and the towns behind, the road would narrow and there would be stretches where the pavement disappeared entirely. During rainstorms, which were rare, it might become impassable, but at the present time their greatest problem should be ruts and potholes deep enough to blow a tire or even snap an axle if a driver did not spot them in advance and cut his speed. Sergeant Ulenga reckoned he could help his partner watch for road hazards along the way, but they were sly and unpredictable.

In fact, Ulenga drove the Volkswagen from Windhoek to Okahandja, forty-odd miles to the north. Its name translates from the Herero language as "The place where two rivers flow into each other to form one wide one." The next town, Otjiwarongo, "Where the fat cattle graze," was the district capital of Namibia's Otjozondjupa Region and the site where German troops had massacred Herero tribesmen by the hundreds in 1904. After topping off the Jetta's fuel tank in Otavi, once a mining center where South Africans defeated German troops in 1915 to secure the district for themselves, the big American took the driver's seat and let Ulenga catch up on his sleep.

As if he could.

Within the past day and a half, his life had been turned upside-down by choices he had made himself. Ulenga wondered whether there was any going back to his career, assuming he survived the mission he had taken on, or if he would be hounded from his homeland as a fugitive.

Despite the chaos back in Windhoek, he assumed that Nampol headquarters must realize that he was out of touch. Namibia had fifteen thousand law-enforcement officers, but fewer than a thousand sergeants. By this time, it stood to reason that headquarters would have tried to reach him, passing orders down the ladder of command, and when Ulenga proved unreachable, inquiries would be made. They could not track him physically—the Nampol budget did not stretch to GPS devices in department cars, much less to the purchase of equipment needed for triangulating cell phones—and he'd left his phone turned off since joining this mission, in any case. Ulenga had not even checked for waiting messages, content to tell himself that he would think about that problem later, when the smoke cleared.

But by that time, it would likely be too late.

Best-case scenario: he faced demotion, probably suspension, possibly dismissal, for dereliction of duty during a crisis. Worst-case, if his superiors found evidence of his involvement in the deadly raids, would be a term of life imprisonment.

Which left him no choice but to flee.

No one who'd seen a prison in Namibia, as he had many times, would voluntarily submit to being caged in one. None of the country's thirteen lockups, rife with AIDS and inmate violence, was fit for human habitation, much less for a lawman who had helped to populate the cells.

Something to think about, as night fell on the highway and concealed the desert stretching on forever past the tunnel of their headlights. Shutting out that view, Sergeant Ulenga closed his eyes and tried to sleep.

BOLAN HAD SEEN worse highways than Namibia's, but he was not complacent. There would be no Auto Club to help out if the Jetta failed, no explanation of their weapons that would satisfy police should an emergency arise. He filled the tank again in Ondangwa, prior to branching off the B1 road onto track that looked more like some of the desert roads he'd driven in America's Southwest, between "towns" that consisted of a gas station, a burger joint and a cheesy tourist trap—someone's idea of a museum or zoo.

Beyond Ondangwa, though, he wouldn't even find that kind of settlement until they crossed the border and were well inside Angola, where he didn't plan to go. Ulenga had their destination narrowed to a two-mile stretch of the Kunene River where he said traffic often crossed without the knowledge of Namibia's border patrol. There was a place where they could hide and watch the river, his companion had explained, then move in closer when they saw the convoy's headlights. Not the best arrangement in the world, but Bolan was an expert at adapting to the circumstances of a given situation. The advantage of surprise was critical. Beyond that, it came down to sheer audacity and skill.

Ulenga sat beside him in the Jetta's shotgun seat, maybe asleep, more likely faking it. He couldn't blame the cop for being nervous, thinking of the life that he had risked—perhaps abandoned—when he cast his lot with Bolan. Second thoughts were inescapable, but they had come too far for Ulenga to decide that it was all a huge mistake. Even if he left Bolan at this stage, the die was cast for him. His best hope, possibly his *only* hope, was to continue with the mission, see it through and hope for victory.

Which would mean what, exactly, for the Nampol sergeant?

Bolan couldn't say, but if they managed to defeat the MLF's Namibian contingent and the men in government who coddled it, Ulenga might acquire some leverage toward saving his career and staying out of jail. Failing that, there was the flight alternative, but would he take it? Would he let Bolan arrange an exit, courtesy of Stony Man Farm, that would resettle him halfway around the world?

Maybe.

It wasn't time to think in those terms yet, but Bolan always did his best to plan ahead. Plotting the future out for someone else was doubly dicey, though, especially when he had only known that someone for a day and change.

The plan that worked for him at the moment: push on and meet the weapons convoy crossing the Kunene, take it out, and see what happened next. If Boavida took the bait from Bolan's phone call, he might help unravel the Mayombe Liberation Front from the inside. If not…

Well, then it meant more work for Bolan, but he'd signed on for a wild ride to the end of the line. Ulenga could decide whether he remained on board, but one thing was predictable, as good as guaranteed.

They hadn't seen the end of bloodshed yet.

Not even close.

**11**

Fanuel Gurirab stared at the two files sitting on his desktop, side by side. Both represented Nampol officers who had been out of touch and absent without leave since the crisis in Windhoek began. An aide had brought the files five minutes earlier, but Gurirab had yet to open either one of them.

*Get on with it,* he told himself. *Stop wasting time!*

He started with the slim manila folder to his left, its index tab bearing the name Shipanga, Kartuutire. Opening the folder, Gurirab discovered that Shipanga was a new recruit with only eighteen months of service on the force. He had departed for a scheduled holiday the afternoon before all hell broke loose and was supposed to be visiting kinfolk in Botswana. So far, three attempts to reach his family by telephone in Ghanzi, at the number he'd provided, had been fruitless.

Meaning what? That they were traveling together, unaware of what had happened—was *still* happening—in Windhoek, totally oblivious to the emergency? Or was Shipanga's holiday part of a finely tuned conspiracy? Had he chosen the dates because he knew trouble was coming and he needed free time to participate? Could it be even worse than that? Was there the slightest possibility that he had joined Nampol more than a year ago already planning these events? Had the recruit used his position on the force to gather information for the killers? Was he now part of their murder spree?

Unfortunately, Gurirab could answer none of those distressing questions. Since he had not located Katuutire Shipanga yet, he had no way of knowing whether the young officer was lolling with his loved ones in the bush somewhere, or stalking members of the MLF around Windhoek.

In short, he had learned nothing.

Muttering a curse, he closed Shipanga's file, pushed it aside and opened up the second, fatter one, which bore the name Ulenga, Sgt. Jakova. The sergeant, he saw, was thirty-one years old. He'd spent eleven years with Nampol after two years in the army, and had been promoted to his present rank in March 2010. Prior to his promotion, Ulenga had served on Nampol's Motor Vehicle Theft Unit and its Crime Investigation Unit. Since promotion he had been assigned to Serious Crimes—which included piracy, gunrunning and human trafficking.

All sources of revenue for the Mayombe Liberation Front.

What did that prove? Nothing, in and of itself.

Where was Sergeant Ulenga at the moment, when he should have been on duty? No one seemed to know.

His last check-in with headquarters was logged approximately fourteen hours earlier—or, put another way, some ninety minutes prior to the attack on Rieckmann Street against the MLF drug lab. Coincidence? More to the point, if he was not involved in the successive incidents, where was Ulenga? Why had he been out of touch this long? Why were the several calls from Nampol headquarters unanswered?

Gurirab had sent an officer to check Ulenga's flat, but no one was at home. Neither, by peering through its windows, could the officer discover any sign of foul play on the premises. Gurirab wondered whether he should send a search team next, ransack the flat for clues, or use some other method to locate his missing sergeant.

And what method would that be? Perhaps a television bulletin: "Sergeant Ulenga, please check in"?

Absurd.

But Gurirab knew that he must try *something,* and he had to do it soon. The thought of harboring a traitor in the ranks unnerved him. And if there were *two* traitors—Ulenga and Shipanga, working as a team—he would have some epic explaining to do.

That prospect made Gurirab's head ache, as he reached out for the telephone.

*The Kunene Rive, Kaokoland, Namibia*

HEADLIGHTS APPROACHING in the distance. Bolan watched them through Ulenga's Opticron pocket binoculars from three miles out, the 8x25 magnification transforming them from tiny fireflies into harbingers of death. Three trucks loaded with military hardware on its way to members of the MLF who would employ the deadly tools in acts of terrorism, piracy and the defense of a criminal syndicate.

Bolan had other ideas.

"We'll let them start across," he said, "then hit them while they're in the water. That should slow down their reaction while we take them, quick and clean."

Ulenga nodded at his side, and Bolan had to wonder if he bought the last part. *Quick and clean* was optimistic—some might say delusional—where any form of combat was concerned. It worked out sometimes, sure, but in the crunch, often as not, things started to unravel and a soldier had to play it all by ear. On instinct.

Their rifles had an effective range of three hundred yards, give or take, but anything approaching accuracy meant they had to cut that distance by two-thirds. Bolan was hoping he could stop the first truck with his GP-30 launcher, then move on to numbers two and three before they started picking off the riders individually. Return fire was a given, but the key advantage of surprise gave them an edge—at least, until his first grenade went off.

Success meant hampering the MLF's war effort and taking a hefty bite out of its treasury. Failure...well, the price of that was constant and unchanging.

If they failed, they died.

The rub: Bolan had no idea how many soldiers would accompany the shipment. Standard military truck cabs seated two men comfortably, but might accommodate three. Extra shooters could ride with the cargo in back, if the trucks weren't chock-full.

Bottom line: it could be a small army, but Bolan was here whatever the reality and ready to rock.

Two miles and closing. Bolan considered last-minute advice, then decided to skip it. Ulenga was a former soldier and policeman, trained and blooded. He knew all the combat basics, and they had no time for schooling in refinements. Bolan's Special Forces training had consumed the best part of a year, forty-eight weeks from start to finish, and he couldn't replicate that ordeal for Ulenga even if he'd wanted to.

So, no pep talk. No pointers. Just a nod to common sense that any cop or soldier should possess if he intended to survive.

Stay low whenever possible. Line up your shots and squeeze—don't jerk—the trigger. Put your target down, no matter what it takes. Forget about "fair" fighting if you want to see another sunrise.

Kill or be killed.

For a man who made his living with a gun, it was the only game in town.

One mile to go, and Bolan was about to lower the binoculars when he picked up a sound from somewhere to his left rear, drawing closer. Engines coming from the wrong direction, at the worst time possible.

Turning, he saw more headlights coming from the south.

LÚCIO JAMBA CURSED THE unpaved road, his driver and the circumstances that had brought him to Kaokoland, otherwise known as the Kunene Region. He was not convinced their enemies would meet the convoy coming from Angola—and if that turned out to be the case, despite his doubts, it was the last place on the planet that he cared to be.

As if he had a choice.

Jamba had spent most of the long drive north considering his options for deposing Boavida. Ordinarily, that end could only be achieved by MLF headquarters, based on charges amply verified. Incompetence, corruption, drunkenness resulting in a loss of soldiers or material would justify removal of an officer, but Jamba had no evidence that would support a court-martial. Instead, he had a vague scheme growing in his mind that could be fatal for him if it failed.

But if he should succeed…

Before there was a hope of that, Jamba had to complete the job that Boavida had assigned to him. Meet the Angolan convoy, help it cross the border without mishap and ensure its safe arrival at the scheduled drop outside of Sesfontein, a former outpost for police who hunted rhino poachers. These days, the settlement—named for its six natural springs, or fountains—served as the capital of Sesfontein Constituency, equivalent to a parliamentary district. The drop outside town, disguised as a mine complete with a hundred-foot shaft, was used for contraband in transit from Angola to end-users in Namibia.

Jamba would see the lorries to their destination, guard them while they were unloaded, then head back to Windhoek while the transports trundled northward, bound for home. It would have been a simple, boring errand under normal circumstances.

But the present circumstances could not pass for normal.

Boavida thought their enemies would meet the convoy and destroy it. Jamba's task was to prevent that interdiction, or to die in the attempt. He wondered if Boavida hoped that he *would* die. Had the man sensed Jamba's ambition and his rising level of distrust for his superior's judgment? Was the trip north meant to be the final journey of his life?

But that would mean that Boavida knew where their opponents would strike next. A mere suspicion left the possibility—even a likelihood—that Jamba would survive. And if the MLF's Namibian commander *knew* the next move of their enemies…then he was one of them.

A traitor to the cause and to his homeland?

Proof of that would justify whatever actions Jamba took against him. But if no such proof existed, might it not be fabricated? What would be required to prove the case and justify Jamba removing Boavida without first consulting headquarters?

Plainly, his word alone was not enough. If there were photographs or documents proving disloyalty, the case would be ironclad. That seemed too much to hope for, but a talent with computers and the latest Photoshop technology should prove invaluable. All Jamba required was background, possibly a photo of the CIA field officer in Windhoek—or the men who were responsible for all the recent carnage.

Even photos of a dead man's face might be enough. And if the men themselves were not available, perhaps another corpse? One thing was certain: a cadaver could not offer any plea in self-defense.

A white man and an African. Why not?

As Jamba's two-car caravan drew close to the Kunene River, he began considering a list of candidates.

"These look like cops to you?" Bolan asked, as he passed Ulenga the field glasses.

After half a minute studying the late-arriving vehicles, Ulenga lowered the binoculars and shook his head. "They're not official vehicles."

"No chance Nampol would bag two private cars in an emergency?"

"None," Ulenga said. "Their equipment may not be the newest or the best available, but there is no shortage of vehicles for back-country patrols."

"Okay, then." Bolan made a mental note that his companion had said *their* equipment, and not *ours*. Without attaching too much psychological significance to that one turn of phrase, he recognized Ulenga's growing separation from the force he served—or *had* served, until recently.

Was that another strike against the Executioner? Had he

taken a good man from his normal life and turned him into something else? Something that could be dark and dangerous?

At this moment in time, the more important thing on Bolan's mind was confirmation that the new arrivals weren't police. Which meant that he had no compunction about killing them.

The pair of dusty SUVs drove past the point where Bolan and Ulenga lay in shadow, in a gully carved by flash floods from a bluff above the river, and proceeded to the southern bank of the Kunene, stopping there. Bolan watched seven men pile out of the two vehicles, all armed. They left the two cars running, high-beam headlights angled north across the river toward Angolan territory.

Welcoming the arms convoy.

If this was the result of Bolan's call to Boavida, he didn't mind. Another seven guns shifted the odds a bit, but not dramatically. Surprise still worked on his side, though he'd have to make a small adjustment in his plan. Instead of dealing with the lead truck first, he'd have to drop a fireball on the soldiers closest to him, on his own side of the river.

At any minute.

His GP-30 was already loaded with a caseless high-explosive round. He made a small adjustment to the weapon's notched quadrant sight, mounted on the right side of the launcher, scaling back some fifteen yards from his original setting. That should drop his first round on the SUV of Bolan's choice to start the party. After that…

"Ready?" he asked Ulenga.

"Yes," the sergeant answered, voice taut with anticipation.

He watched the first truck in the convoy pull up to the northern riverbank. Its headlights flashed, the driver waiting for an answer. When it came, he eased his hulking vehicle into the water, grinding forward in low gear. The second truck in line waited until the first had crossed halfway, then followed.

"Here we go," Bolan said.

As he spoke, he aimed and fired the GP-30 with his left hand, held his AK-47 steady as the VOG-25P frag round arced downrange toward impact. A second later, it struck the tailgate of the SUV on Bolan's left and detonated in a thunderclap, slamming the vehicle forward and lighting a fat ball of fire at its rear. The fuel tank blew next, spewing brilliant streamers that set fire to everything they touched—gunmen, the second SUV, the river's bank and the Kunene snaking past.

So much for the surprise. Only sudden death remained.

IT IS A RULE OF FIREFIGHTING that water cannot douse a petroleum blaze. A fire lit with gasoline or similar accelerants cannot be drowned; it must be smothered, starved for oxygen by chemicals or by some object physically impervious to flame.

Still, when the SUV to Jamba's right exploded, spraying him with liquid fire, he did not stop to ponder what he had been taught in safety class at school so long ago. His crackling, scalded face and scalp shrieked at him first, a bolt of white-hot misery, before the blazing fuel ate through his shirt, into his arm, shoulder and back. Screaming in agony, Jamba did all that he could think of in that moment. Lurching forward, he plunged into the Kunene River's flow and sank.

Relief was instantaneous, but tragically short-lived. The water *did* smother the flames tormenting Jamba, but a heartbeat later it washed over nerves exposed and sparking from destruction of his epidermis by the flash fire that had nearly killed him. And it might still kill him, Jamba realized, if he went into shock and let the river carry him away to some point where he'd sink a second time, and doubtless drown.

Sobbing, one-eyed, Jamba struggled toward dry land. He veered off from the burning SUVs, the lorry that had detonated with its own apocalyptic *BANG!!!* mere seconds later, while he was submerged and sucking water in with every gargled scream. Gunfire was crackling back and forth between the convoy and a party of attackers on the south side of the river. Muzzle-flashes vaguely registered with Jamba, while the *pop-pop-pop* of firing mingled with the raging static in his half-fried head.

Before he reached the riverbank, it struck Jamba that he had not lost his rifle. When he tried to flex the fingers clutching it, new pain lanced up his arm, and Jamba realized his palm was melted to the gun somehow. If he could not release it, he could not defend himself, could not exact revenge against the bastards who had left him scarred and suppurating in the desert night.

Somehow, he reached the water's edge, collapsed there, dropping to his knees, then rolling over on his left side to avoid contact between his raw flesh and the soil. Wheezing through seared lips, Jamba took stock of his condition.

He was still alive, if only just. His suffering proved that. And he could move, although the crisped skin on his right side bled and crackled when he did so, flooding him with waves of pain that threatened his consciousness. His first job, Jamba knew, was to control his weapon—or at least find out if it was functional.

Cursing and groaning without respite, Jamba wedged the AK-47's stock between his trembling knees, then brought his left hand to his right and started peeling his fried fingers from the rifle's pistol grip. Each finger that released the weapon left seared flesh behind, protesting with new jolts of agony, but Jamba kept on at the task until his hand was free.

Next all he had to do was stand, switch hands to fire the piece left-handed, awkward as it might be, and move out to find his enemies. To kill them for this thing that they had done to him.

And if he died a heartbeat after finishing the last of them, so be it.

Jamba thought it might be a relief.

BOLAN RAISED THE GP-30's sight and sent another HE round hurtling across the river, toward the third truck in the convoy, scored a hit atop its hood, and saw the windshield vanish in a burst of smoke and flame. That took the driver and his shotgun rider out of action, but a third man leaped out of the truck's rear bed, splashed down in the Kunene, and went churning back the way they'd come from, toward Angola's side.

Take him, or let him go?

Why let an enemy escape to fight another day, when it could mean another act of terrorism targeting civilians or legitimate authorities?

Bolan lined up the shot and fired a 3-round burst from his Kalashnikov, dropping the runner in mid stream. The current took his target, sweeping him away and out of sight westward, as the Executioner turned back to living adversaries.

Fifteen feet away, to Bolan's right, Ulenga raked the river's bank and burning SUVs with measured bursts from his AKMS carbine, picking and choosing targets from the reinforcements who'd arrived in time to die after a long drive from the south. Bolan swung toward the convoy's second truck, sandwiched between two smoking hulks, and fed another caseless round into the 30's muzzle, felt the spring catch clasp it, then aimed quickly and squeezed off, lobbing one more dose of death into the night.

The middle truck shuddered on impact, as the flat roof of its cab peeled back, a fiery storm of shrapnel taking out its occupants. Maybe they screamed, but Bolan couldn't hear it over all the other noise of combat roaring in his ears. Another rifleman bailed out behind, and got no farther than the other had, as Bolan's AK tracked him, zeroed on his back and brought him down.

All that remained was mopping up. A quick scan of the riverbank showed Bolan one man standing—more or less standing. The figure lurched and staggered, struggled to remain upright—and seemed to be trailing smoke, or steam. It grappled with a weapon, borne left-handed in an awkward grip, the right hand flinching back repeatedly from contact with the rifle. Bolan guessed it was one of the late arrivals, caught up in the firestorm that his first grenade unleashed.

A little taste of hell on earth.

He sympathized with any suffering, but did not let it sway him. This was war, and war meant killing, as some long-forgotten general had said, somewhere behind him in the mists of time. A man who didn't recognize that basic truth had no damned business carrying a weapon into combat in the first place.

Bolan could have gone to meet his last surviving adversary on the riverbank, but what would be the point? High noon was still twelve hours off, and they were half a world away from Hollywood. He framed the shambling figure in his AK's sights and stuttered off four rounds to finish the job.

On the Kunene, fire had found the ammunition and explosives packed aboard the trucks. The echo of their rapid-fire explosions followed Bolan and Ulenga on the walk through sand dunes to the Jetta, and their long drive back to Windhoek's urban battleground.

**12**

*Mayombe Liberation Front Headquarters, Windhoek*

Boavida was expecting Jamba to call as soon as the man had reached a point where cell phone links were possible. Instead, the voice addressing him belonged to a Detective Constable Nangolo Esau, who spoke almost mechanically as he recited Boavida's private number.

"May I ask to whom I'm speaking, sir?"

Suspicious, Boavida thought about the question for a moment, then decided there could be no harm in giving up his name. He was already known to Nampol officers above the caller's rank, and had some of the most important on retainer.

"Oscar Boavida," he admitted, finally.

"And, sir, are you familiar with a Mr. Lúcio Jamba?"

Disturbed, Boavida answered with a question of his own. "Why do you ask, Detective?"

"Mr. Boavida, I'm afraid I have bad news for you."

Of course. What other kind was there these days?

"And what would that be?" Boavida asked the stranger who was calling him at—check the time for reference—3:19 a.m. in the morning. He pictured a freak auto accident, Jamba in custody. Christ, had he been driving drunk? Had the weapons been found?

"Sir, I regret to tell you that Mr. Jamba is dead…along with fifteen other men whom we are trying to identify."

The floor tilted beneath him, might have toppled Boavida if he had not been sitting on the edge of his bed with the phone at his ear. Even so, he felt a giddy sense of vertigo, approaching nausea. It took a Herculean effort to control his voice, and Boavida wasn't altogether sure that he had managed it.

"Fifteen, you say?" Remembering in time to act confused. "But…where? What happened?"

"We're still sorting out the details, sir. Did Mr. Jamba live in Windhoek?"

"Yes," Boavida said. "Where are you, if I may ask?"

"Calling from Opuwo, sir."

"Opuwo? But I don't… What was he doing in Opuwo?"

"I was hoping that you might tell me, sir," Detective Esau said.

"No. I mean, I couldn't say. He didn't mention leaving Windhoek when we spoke last."

"When was that, sir?" the officer asked.

"Yesterday morning, half-past eight o'clock or so," Boavida said. "Lúcio called me to say he wasn't feeling well and wouldn't be at work today."

"What is his work, sir?"

"I am a political consultant," Boavida answered, sticking to the vague title that graced his cut-rate business cards. If necessary, he could offer references. "He is…he *was* my office manager."

"Do you have any thoughts on why he might be here in Kaokoland?" the detective asked.

"No."

"Or why he might be traveling with six armed men, as it appears, to meet a train of lorries coming from Angola, filled with weapons?"

"What? I don't… What are you saying?" Boavida gave himself top marks for feigned confusion. It was no great challenge, this projecting of emotion, when his stomach roiled with acid threatening to eat him from the inside out. "Weapons? You're not making sense, Detective."

"I'm afraid it is the facts that don't make sense, sir," Esau countered. "For an office manager, at least."

Boavida let a hint of anger creep into his tone. "I can't explain what Lúcio was doing in Kaokoland, Detective. All our clients live and work in Windhoek—in the Parliament, the Ministry of Home Affairs and so on. As for weapons and armed men, let me assure you they play no part in our work."

"Very good, sir," Detective Esau said. "I have no doubt someone from the ministry you mentioned will be calling you for further details later on today. Meanwhile, I hope you will accept my personal condolence on the loss of your...assistant."

"Yes. If I could tell you any more—"

"Good night, sir," the detective interrupted Boavida, and the line went dead.

Like Jamba and the others. All of them. Sixteen including Jamba, and all the weapons lost.

And then it struck him.

If there was a traitor in the ranks, as his white caller had warned Boavida earlier, it could not have been Jamba. Why in hell would he contrive to kill himself?

But if the traitor *wasn't* Jamba...

Who else could Boavida trust?

EVEN WITH THE BATTLEGROUND a hundred miles behind them as they drove through the Omusati Region, Bolan still watched out for Nampol vehicles behind them, or approaching from the east. It was still dark out—two hours until dawn, officially—so there was no point checking overhead for aircraft. Nampol's airwing had been created in 2009, and had waited twelve months longer for its second helicopter to arrive.

Two choppers to cover eight hundred and twenty-five thousand square miles?

Bolan reckoned they had a good chance of evading that team.

The flip side of that coin was desolate country with only six recognized highways. The state, in its wisdom, had dubbed them B1 through B8, with no B5 or B7 to fill out the list. Lesser roads—meaning one lane with dubious pavement—had a C prefix, with double-digit numbers. The worst routes available, unpaved and rarely maintained, carried a D prefix and four-digit numbers.

Namibia has no A-rated roads.

If they were spotted on their journey back to Windhoek, Bolan had no realistic hope that his Volkswagen could outrun a Nampol cruiser. And for damn sure, he would find no place to hide from searchers in a landscape that was mostly desert, with a few scrub trees along the way to offer minimal variety. Their only hope lay in avoiding the police as long as possible and hoping they could reach the crowded city without being stopped.

So far, so good.

"You know," Ulenga said, breaking the silence that had stretched for thirty miles, "there will be more weapons next week, next month, whenever."

"Sure there will," Bolan agreed. "First thing you learn in this business, there's no such thing as final victory. A battle's only won *for now*. You stick around in one place long enough, you'll have to do it all over again, from scratch."

"And if you don't stay?" Ulenga asked, sounding vaguely wistful.

"Same thing, different scenery," Bolan replied. "It doesn't matter if you're in Namibia, in Russia or the States. Look past their pigment and their dialect, people are all the same. Most people do their best, while some hang back and prey on the majority. They may use politics or a religion as their cover— some may even be sincere, who knows? But the results don't vary. People who've done nothing to the predators still wind up dead or wounded, homeless, violated. Traumatized."

"But if you cannot stop it…"

"What's the point? I still ask that, from time to time," the Executioner admitted.

"And can you answer?" Ulenga asked.

"Likely not to anybody's satisfaction but my own," Bolan said. "I can't save the world, okay? Hell, I can't even save a town the size of Windhoek. Any long-term change depends on locals rising up, demanding that their leaders either solve a problem or step down in favor of someone who will. Finding a true reformer isn't easy. I'm not sure I've ever met one."

"Then it's all a waste of time," Ulenga said.

"Might look that way," Bolan acknowledged. "But consider

this—if you're a villager and there's a crocodile that hangs out at your water hole, eating whoever comes along, what do you do? Pack up and move? Let it keep snacking on your neighbors?"

"Kill it," Ulenga said.

"There you go," Bolan said. "But you always know another croc may come along and start the same thing all over again."

"Sometimes," Ulenga told him, staring out the window into darkness, "I prefer the crocodiles."

"I hear you," Bolan said. "You and me, both."

*Cuban Embassy, Windhoek*

CAPTAIN RODRIGO ACOSTA was accustomed to strange hours. The nature of his work dictated that he be ready and available to deal with problems as they came, at any hour of the day or night. It could be anything: a summons from a worried diplomat demanding information or a wounded agent seeking refuge from local authorities. Whatever the demand, he must respond promptly, professionally—with, it hardly needed saying, one eye firmly fixed on the preservation and advancement of his own career.

This morning it was Boavida, calling once again with more complaints about the losses he had suffered from attacks by unknown enemies. Since one of those, a faceless white man, was presumed by some to be American, Acosta had attempted to identify him with the tools at his disposal, but the task had proved fruitless. In the wake of 9/11, the United States simply had too many competing agencies involved in covert work around the world: collection of intelligence, "rendition" and "enhanced interrogation" of suspected terrorists, attacks on suspect individuals and groups which ranged from surgical removal to the deployment of the Reaper drones most famous for near-misses in Afghanistan and Pakistan.

Too many agencies and far too many hunters on the loose these days.

On top of which, Acosta was not absolutely certain that his target was American, or even acting on behalf of a specific government. It was a fact of life that Boavida and the MLF had enemies, in Africa and elsewhere.

"What have you learned?" Boavida asked, after a truncated salutation. Courtesy had never been his strong point, and the rudeness grated on Acosta's Latin sensibilities.

"So far, nothing," Acosta answered.

"What? *Nothing?* How is that possible?"

"Review the circumstances, Oscar. You asked me to find a white man, reasonably tall and possibly American. Beyond that, you provided no description, certainly no name or other leads to his identity."

"But you—"

Acosta interrupted him to say, "On my initiative, inquiries have been made at Hosea Kutako International. As you're aware, it is the only airport in the country that accepts international flights."

"Yes, yes. But—"

"In the week before your trouble started, fifteen white men, traveling alone, landed at the airport. According to their passports—which, you realize, may have been forged—six of the men were German, three British, two French, two from the United States, one Russian, and one Greek. At my suggestion, the police have launched inquiries to discover which of those are still inside Namibia, and where they may be found."

"With what result?" Boavida asked, managing to sound slightly impressed.

"Of the fifteen," Acosta said, "nine left within two days of their arrival—five Germans, both Frenchmen, the Russian, and one American. That leaves—"

"Yes, I can count!" The rudeness coming back again. "Where are the rest?"

Acosta made his caller wait ten seconds, while he calmed himself, then said, "Inquiries are ongoing. As you know, all visitors must proffer an address where they'll be staying in Namibia. In each case, the remaining six listed hotels—five here in Windhoek, one in Swakopmund. That is the Greek vice president of a respected shipping company and fifty-nine years old. Police in Swakopmund confirm his presence there. He's not your man."

"Still, five remain," Boavida said. "That is something."

"There is more," Acosta told him. "I've discovered through a contact with FSB in Moscow that the Russian is a wealthy businessman with one foot in the underworld. It's possible, in my opinion, that he may attempt to deal with your competitors for access to specific contraband, but he is not a soldier. Furthermore, one of your local officers assigned to Interpol has shadowed him since his arrival in Namibia. Again, he's not your man."

Growing impatient, Boavida pressed him. "What of the American?"

Acosta paused again, refusing to be hurried. "Police confirm two of the Englishmen pursuing normal business here in Windhoek," he forged on. "The third was not at his hotel, the Heinitzburg, when they checked in. They will keep looking for him. The last German divides his time between discussions with a local manufacturer and dallying with prostitutes. He has no time for killing revolutionaries."

"The American!" Boavida exclaimed.

"*Sí*. The name on his passport is Matt Cooper. Home address in Richmond, Virginia—a street that exists, by the way, in an affluent suburb. He travels on business, unstated, and lists his address as the Hotel Furstenhof on Dr. Frans Indongo Street. A room has been reserved there, in his name. Again, he was not present when police came calling."

"You have a description?"

While Acosta gave it to him, he heard Boavida scrawling notes. Finished, he said, "Your immigration officers, regrettably, do not photocopy passports."

"They're not *my* officers," said Boavida. "Not my people."

"Yet you stay."

"What will you do now?" Boavida asked him.

"Do? What can I do?" Acosta countered. "It is up to the police, or to the men you call your soldiers. But whatever you intend to do, for your own sake, I'd recommend you do it soon."

ULENGA WOKE WITH A START, surprised that he'd managed to doze while Bolan drove through the early-morning darkness. Far off to the east, a faint gray line marked the horizon and the advent of another scorching day.

"I'm sorry if I snored," Ulenga said.

"I've heard worse," Bolen assured him. "We're ten minutes out of Otjiwarongo."

Another stop for fuel, Ulenga thought, before they crossed over to the Khomas Region and the last leg of their journey back to Windhoek. Back to battle once again with the May-ombe Liberation Front.

"What will we do next, Cooper?" Ulenga asked.

"Blow a few more houses down, then pay a call on Boa-vida," he replied.

"He'll be well-guarded."

"Probably. The good news is, we've whittled down his army and he'll have them spread thin on the ground, covering any place we've missed so far."

"And when he's dead," Ulenga said, "then that's the end of it?"

"For him, at least," Bolan said. "The MLF won't fold its tent unless Namibian authorities crack down on it across the board. We haven't even scratched the surface of its operations in Angola, where the leadership comes from."

"You're going to Angola next?"

The big American shook his head. "Not this time out," he said. "But I may drop in to see some of the folks who've been helping the MLF on this side of the border."

Where would that lead him? Ulenga thought the tall Ameri-can could lose himself pursuing everyone who'd given aid to Oscar Boavida and his men, from ministers of government down to Nampol patrolmen on the street.

"You may be here forever at that rate," he said.

"Not if I do it right," Bolan said. "You can't touch all the bases, necessarily, but touch the right ones, and the message comes across."

Ulenga understood, or thought he did. The warrior had a brief to follow, laid down by the people who had sent him to

Namibia, and possibly a time limit for the performance of his task. In which case…

"You'll be leaving soon, then?"

"If it all works out, sooner rather than later," he replied. "And what about yourself? Have you made any plans for afterward?"

"It's difficult," Ulenga said. "I have a passport and a little money put away, if I can reach it. Otherwise—"

"The money shouldn't be a problem," Bolan suggested, "with the stash we took from Boavida's club on Prum Street."

Taken by surprise, Ulenga turned to face his partner. "Don't you need that for yourself?"

"I brought plenty," he replied, "and I don't plan on any shopping. If it helps to get you started over somewhere safe, it's yours."

And underneath his gratitude, Ulenga thought, *I'm also a thief, not just a murderer.*

The faint gray streak of dawn did no more than the lights of Otjiwarongo, visible before them, to pierce the darkness that he felt lurking inside himself.

"I'd like to check on my apartment," Ulenga said. "I can take my own car, when we reach Windhoek."

"It could be dangerous," Bolan said.

"I won't be long," Ulenga said. He closed his eyes once more, and wondered where this long strange ride would end.

FANUEL GURIRAB ENJOYED waking the Deputy Assistant Minister of Home Affairs before daylight had brightened Windhoek's streets. He sat and waited while a servant fetched Moses Kaujeua to the telephone. As to the nature of his call, there was no pleasure in it. Rather, Gurirab suspected that he might be damned for treachery.

Of course, the man he was betraying had already broken faith with him, with Nampol. And, as the Americans were fond of saying, payback is a bitch.

"Hello?" Kaujeua's voice was throaty, gruff. "I trust you have good reason for a call at this ungodly hour, Captain."

"Yes, sir. It appears one of our officers may be involved in these attacks in Windhoek, at Durissa Bay and up in Kaoko-land."

"What's that? Another one up north? When did that happen?" Kaujeua asked.

"Around midnight, sir. Another bad one. Sixteen dead, three lorries filled with weapons from Angola."

"Christ on Friday!" Having blurted out the curse, Kaujeua caught himself and asked, "Does this mean that the men responsible are leaving? Have they crossed the border?"

"We have nothing to suggest it, sir. And if an officer from Windhoek is involved, it stands to reason that he'll come back here."

"Police involved in terrorism. How can such a thing occur?" Kaujeua challenged.

"Sir, our officers are only human, as you know," Gurirab said. "Some steal. Two were dismissed in January for molesting women they'd arrested. Anything is possible."

"But this?"

"If I was forced to speculate," Gurirab said, "I might suggest, sir, that the officer may not regard his actions as those of a terrorist."

"But what else would you call it?" the Deputy Assistant Minister asked.

"If he had been assigned to watch the MLF, sir, and grew tired of seeing crimes ignored or minimized, he might see what he's doing as a form of justice."

"Vigilantism? It's still the same as terrorism," Kaujeua said.

"To us, perhaps," Gurirab said, thinking, *To you.* "But to a dedicated, frustrated policeman, I am not so sure."

"Don't tell me that you sympathize with this." It came out sounding like an order, rather than a question.

"No, sir. Absolutely not. But I can understand it," Gurirab replied.

"Less understanding, Captain, and more action. Can you find this rogue or not?"

"We're searching for him, sir, of course. He's not at home, but otherwise..."

"Give me his name and address," Kaujeua said, "and I'll see what I can do."

Gurirab hesitated, then obeyed, waiting until Kaujeua wrote the name of Sergeant Jakova Ulenga down, then spelled it back to him. The address next, for an apartment house on Korrthaan Street, in Tauben Glen. Again it was repeated to him, first the number, then the street name.

"Yes, sir. That's correct," Gurirab said.

"All right, I have it," Kaujeua said. "Make no further efforts to contact him there, you understand?"

"Yes, sir." Gurirab understood that he'd condemned a fellow Nampol officer to death if he was found at home. "Shall we continue looking for him elsewhere, then?"

"Of course," Kaujeua said. "I'm sure you will agree that we must stop this rampage by whatever means may be available."

*Including murder,* Captain Gurirab supposed.

He said, "Yes, sir. Agreed."

"You've done your duty, Captain," the Second Deputy Assistant Minister for Home Affairs said. "Rest easy in that knowledge."

"As you say, sir."

And the line went dead.

*Rest easy?*

*No,* Gurirab thought. *That was not in the cards.*

**13**

Ulenga drove his Opel Corsa south on Hendrik Witbooi Drive to Pelican Street, turned east when he got there, and made his way to the Tauben Glen suburb. It was an upscale neighborhood, expensive homes, but some of them had been converted to apartment houses. So it was with his address on Korrthaan Street, a house with five bedrooms where tenants shared the kitchen and the former single-family home's two bathrooms.

Not the best arrangement, granted, but he could have paid much higher rent for a similar place in Windhoek Central, or saved money on a rat-infested dump in South Industrial. Having a Nampol officer in residence also relieved some of the live-in landlord's personal anxiety, and shaved a little off Ulenga's monthly tab.

A part of him was sad to lose the apartment, but what choice did he have? After his strange adventure with Matt Cooper, logic dictated there could be no going back to normal service as a law-enforcement officer. Assuming that the force would even take him back, instead of prosecuting him and jailing him for life, Ulenga knew that the frustration he had felt before the past day and a half would only be amplified a thousand times.

Would be unbearable, in fact.

The first thing he must do, Ulenga thought, was choose a place to live outside Namibia. Perhaps outside Africa. He thought of South America, a climate more or less the same as he was used to, but he knew nothing of the immigration policies its several nations followed. Could Matt Cooper or his employers help with that? he wondered. Was Jakova Ulenga doomed to spend his whole life leaning on the big American?

First money—which, in truth, Ulenga would be happy to accept—and next he was confronted by a basic ignorance of how things worked outside Namibia, or Africa at large. Of course, he knew the rudiments of travel, setting up a household, but when they were finished this mission, if they lived that long, Ulenga would become a stateless person. He would have to settle somewhere, go through all the red tape that surrounded immigration, and it might not suit him by the time he finished jumping through a hundred bureaucratic hoops.

Too bad, he thought. You made your choice, you have to live with it.

Assuming they—the MLF, Nampol, whomever—let him live.

With that in mind, Ulenga turned into the eastern end of Korrthaan Street and followed it southeast to Perihuhn. A casual inspection of the street revealed no Nampol vehicles, but would they be that obvious?

A stakeout team could commandeer a neighbor's house, or might be waiting in his own apartment, with their cars tucked somewhere out of sight.

All that assumed that headquarters had worked out his involvement in the Windhoek raids. It was just as likely, he supposed, that someone in the personnel department had declared him simply absent without leave during the crisis. There was no good reason for them to suspect him, on the face of it. Perhaps, when all the smoke cleared, if he was alive, he'd merely face suspension or dismissal for dereliction of duty.

In which case, he need not leave Windhoek at all.

Ulenga thought that he could find another job, however menial, and stash the money he received from Cooper while taking time to plan a leisurely, well-thought-out exit from the city and his homeland. If he was not forced to rush, fleeing from prosecution or assassination, everything would be much easier.

And he could do it on his own, without any help.

But first, he felt the need to look around his flat, find out if anyone had been there looking for him—and, if so, whether he could divine their motive and intentions.

To do that, of course, he had to turn around, go back and find a place to park the Opel, then go on inside. Ulenga knew he would be vulnerable from the moment that he parked his car, but he could not drive off and leave his flat, all his belongings, without one more look around.

Call it a salvage run.

He circled north and east on Perihuhn Street, coming back to Korrthaan. Pausing at the intersection for a slow, deep breath, Ulenga turned west once again and started looking for a parking spot.

AFTER DROPPING OFF ULENGA at his car and setting up a time for them to rendezvous downtown, Bolan drove northwest on Florence Nightingale and wound his way from there into the Windhoek suburb known as Khomasdal. Its centerpiece appeared to be a soccer stadium, but Bolan's interest lay elsewhere, specifically on Borgward Street, where the Mayombe Liberation Front maintained an office on the order of a numbers bank run by the syndicate at home, collecting bets and making the occasional payoff on an unlicensed lottery.

His plan was simple—hit and git, enhancing Ulenga's getaway fund with another MLF donation before they called it a day. Whatever happened next, it was unlikely that they'd find another opportunity to profit from the game as it played out.

The place was decked out as a pawn shop, possibly appropriate for gamblers fallen on hard times. When Bolan entered from the street, two burly figures with dramatic hair—dreadlocks on one, cornrows atop the other—eyeballed him suspiciously from where they stood behind a showcase filled with rings and other jewelry.

"Help you?" the man wearing cornrows asked.

"Absolutely," Bolan said. "I need a loan."

"So, what we talkin' 'bout?" the other man asked.

"Depends," Bolan replied. "How much is in the safe?"

The pair swapped glances, and the first man said, "The loan depends on what you pawn."

"Okay," Bolan said, drawing the Beretta with its silencer attached. "Let's call it a withdrawal, then."

"You crazy, man?" the second man asked.

"It's been said," Bolan assured him. "Best for you if you don't test the diagnosis."

The man with the cornrows made the first move, left hand yanking up his shirttail while his right went for the pistol tucked inside the waistband of his trousers. Bolan put a round beneath his stubbled chin, punching a clean hole through his larynx, severing his spine near its connection to the skull. The shooter dropped as if his skeleton had suddenly evaporated, limp and dead before he hit the floor.

The man with the dreadlocks was frozen in the middle of a slow, aborted draw. "Hey, man," he said. "You want the money, tha's awright by me."

"Good thinking," Bolan said. "Toss the gun away, left-handed, and we'll get our business done."

The man obeyed, making no move that would invite a Parabellum round. Disarmed, he led Bolan to a spacious room in back, where a card table was piled with betting slips around a calculator. The safe sat in a corner, waist-high and speckled with rust.

"Suppose I didn't know the combination?" the man asked.

"I guess you're out of luck," Bolan said.

"Yeah. Just checkin', man."

He knelt before the safe, shielding the combination dial with his broad torso as he spun it, as if that made any difference. Maybe it helped him feel as if he wasn't giving in completely. Bolan didn't know and didn't care. Inside the safe sat stacks of cash, bundled with rubber bands. Bolan had no idea how much was there, but meant to have it all.

"I'll need a bag for that," he said.

"Should be one in the desk. You want me get it?"

"Go ahead," Bolan replied.

The man stood up, crossed to the desk, opened a drawer that would be on the bottom-right if he were seated in the low-backed swivel chair. His quick eyes telegraphed the thought of treachery before he reached inside the drawer, and Bolan shot him through his cranium, punching the corpse back toward collision with a row of filing cabinets.

Inside the drawer, a Browning Hi-Power autoloader lay atop the folded fake-leather satchel he was looking for. Bolan removed the gun and left it on the desktop, took the bag and filled it with the money from the safe, closing the zipper with considerable effort once he had it stuffed with the currency.

He'd let Ulenga count it later, maybe on the road that took him to a brand-new life.

Meanwhile, the old one wasn't finished yet. And if the Executioner got careless, it could go out with a bang.

DAMIÃO MATOS SAW the Opel start to make its second pass and said, in Portuguese, "I think it's him."

"How can you tell?" Mário Cardoso asked from the back-seat of their Mitsubishi Lancer. "See, the windscreen's filthy."

"Here, I have the photograph," their driver, Jonas Rafael, said, taking the passport-size photo from his breast pocket and hand it to Matos in the shotgun seat.

Matos peered closely at the photograph, then turned back to the Opel, but it had already passed them, slowing as its driver found a parking space along the curb. One of the Opel's brake lights flickered as he stopped, preparing to parallel park.

"A short-circuit," Rafael said. "He ought to fix that."

"Does it matter?" Matos asked.

"I guess not."

"Get ready," Matos said, to his two companions.

And obeyed his own order, checking the safety on the Uzi Pro that he held cradled in his lap. A modernized version of the Micro-Uzi machine pistol, the Uzi Pro retained its parent weapon's blowback-operated, closed-bolt, select-fire action, but features a side-mounted bolt handle. Its pistol grip and trigger housing had been redesigned for two-handed action and fabricated from polymer to reduce the original's weight. Four integral Picatinny rails allowed attachment of various sights and other accessories, but Matos had not customized his man-shredder.

Cardoso and Rafael both carried AKS-74U rifles, the shortest Kalashnikovs available at 19.3 inches with stocks folded, but they still looked oversized in comparison to Matos's machine pistol at 11.1 inches. Size *did* matter, at least for concealment, but any one of the weapons could take out their target this morning.

Assuming they had the right man.

The Opel's driver spent close to five minutes parking his old dusty car. When he was satisfied at last, he spent another moment sitting there, perhaps deciding whether it was safe for him to make a move. Or maybe he'd forgotten something on his shopping list, if this was the wrong man. Their orders were to watch the target's flat, not follow suspects here and there around Windhoek.

"Come on, *otario*," Cardoso muttered from the backseat. "We haven't got all day to sit and watch a *paneleiro* daydreaming."

But when the new arrival moved, he managed to surprise them. Where a driver normally would exit through his own door, this one slid across the Opel's seat to climb out on the passenger's side, thereby keeping his face averted as he closed the door and moved away from them, along the sidewalk.

*"Merda!"* Rafael cursed. "What now?"

"Just wait," Matos said. "Find out where he's going."

They already knew the target's address, had been staring at the red facade of the apartment house for two long hours. If the Opel's driver chose another door, he could not be their man.

"I can't tell if he's armed," Rafael said.

"Could have a pistol underneath that shirt," Cardoso guessed.

The same way that they each carried theirs.

Matos sat watching, silently, until the Opel's driver made

his choice, turned off the sidewalk, moving toward the red apartment house with quick, sure strides.

"It *is* him." Rafael was fairly crowing.

"Or another tenant," Matos said.

"What, coming home this early in the morning?"

"From a night job," Matos said. "Or partying at some *bordel*."

"What, you don't want it to be him?" Cardoso challenged.

"*Idiota.* I don't want to kill the wrong man by mistake and pay the price for it," Matos replied. "If he's the one we want, he'll be inside the right apartment, eh?"

"*Número cinco,*" Rafael contributed.

"Right," Matos agreed, just as the Opel's driver entered the apartment house and closed its door behind him. "Now, are you two coming with me, or must I do this alone?"

WHEN BOAVIDA'S CELL PHONE rang, he almost did not answer it. The MLF's Namibian commander felt that he had reached a point where one more piece of bad news might just send him screaming through headquarters with a weapon in his hand, firing at anyone he met along the way.

But, no.

He drew back from the sharp edge of hysteria, picked up the phone and opened it, although reluctantly.

"Hello?"

"You've heard the news by now, I guess," the too-familiar voice intoned. "From up north, that would be."

"You call me now to gloat?" The bitter taste in Boavida's throat reminded him of bile.

"To tell you that it just gets worse from here on in," the caller said. "You have too many enemies to walk away from this, unless you leave right now."

The bark of laughter startled Boavida, coming as it did from his own lips. "Leave and go *where?*" he asked the stranger. "To Angola? Where I tell them…what? That I was frightened by a white man on the telephone?"

"Your call. I'd pick another place, if I were you."

"I still have work to do in Windhoek," Boavida said, no longer caring if the line was tapped, his words being recorded.

"Okay," the caller said. "It's your funeral."

"Not only mine," Boavida said. "Who will save your little friend from Nampol, eh?"

Dead silence on the other end rewarded and encouraged him. The information he'd been given must be accurate, or else the phantom caller would be laughing at him. Instead, the white man answered, "Anything you do from this point on just digs a deeper hole."

"And that should matter, why?" Boavida asked. "If I'm doomed, as you've already said, why should I make it easy for you?"

"Easy, hard, it's all the same. Whichever way it plays, you're done."

"So your CIA proclaimed during the war for independence in Angola. Where are they today?" Boavida asked. "Your consular officials come with hats in hand to beg for oil."

"I'm not a diplomat," the caller answered. "And for whatever it's worth, I'm not affiliated with the Company."

"And if I don't believe you?"

"Doesn't matter," the stranger said. "It goes down the same, regardless."

"And for your comrade, too. Sergeant Ulenga, is it?" Boavida listened for a catch of breath, heard nothing, so he forged ahead. "You think he can survive this? Now that he is known? Even in prison for his many crimes, do you believe he will be safe?"

"Can't say I recognize the name," the caller said. "But you've been warned. Unless you leave Namibia today, you're dead."

And so, a second later, was the line. Boavida cut off the buzzing dial tone, closed his cell phone and laid it aside with a trembling hand. Standing up to the caller had cost him. He felt drained of energy, but his fear had receded.

And why?

Had the promise of death stiffened up his resolve, or simply removed any doubt of the battle's outcome? Either way, he'd been truthful in telling the caller that he, Boavida, had no-where to run.

Angola was closed to him if he tried to go home a defeated, pathetic failure. His own superiors would have him killed as an example to their other warriors, reinforcing their deter-mination to keep up the struggle. If he stayed and fought in Windhoek, then it might be possible for Boavida to redeem his honor.

Failing that, at least he would not have to face himself again and see his shame reflected in a mirror.

Even that was something, after all.

ULENGA FELT NERVOUS, exposed, on the walk from his car to the porch of his lodging house. The feeling eased a little once he was inside, the door shut behind him. But he knew that danger might be waiting for him up the stairs, inside his flat. It would be easy for a stakeout team—or anyone, for that matter—to penetrate the house and set a trap, waiting for his return.

The house was quiet, but the time of day explained that. All his neighbors would be at work. There were no children in the place, and all the tenants worked long hours to make ends meet. Some held two jobs, were rarely seen. Ulenga had no qualms about drawing his pistol as he climbed the stairs to reach the second floor.

He half expected someone to be waiting for him on the landing there, prepared to ambush him, but he found himself still alone. Ulenga felt a bit more confident as he proceeded to his flat, paused at the door, and switched the weapon to his left hand while he rummaged in a pocket for his key. Thinking *I should have had it ready,* when he found it, looked both ways along the hall once more, then braced himself.

The key turned easily, as always. There was no explo-sion as he cracked the door, paused listening, then pushed it open with his pistol raised. No movement in the one room he called home. The great advantage of a small flat was its lack of hiding places for an enemy.

Ulenga crossed the threshold, finally remembering to breathe, and locked the door behind him. Moving toward the closet, he retrieved a small suitcase and placed it on the bed, open, as he went back to fetch his clothes. The bag would hold most of them, he'd decided, since he had no further need for any of his Nampol uniforms or their accessories.

Where would he be, this time the next day, when his work with the big American was finished? Maybe on an airplane flying from Hosea Kutako International to…where? His mind still balked at choosing destinations, making any long-range plans. It was too difficult to see beyond the afternoon. Beyond what must be done.

More killing, certainly. The MLF would not retire without a fight. Cooper recognized that fact and made no bones about it. He had offered yet another chance for Ulenga to leave—while the "getting was good," as he put it—but he had declined. He had not come this far and given up the only life he'd ever known, to turn and run away before the end.

A bitter end, no doubt. Even victorious, if such a thing was possible for two men facing down an army. They could hardly celebrate. At some point even victory rang hollow, had a sour taste about it. In the army, he had felt the same thing. Doing "good," however that was legally defined, might not bring any great sense of accomplishment. In fact, sometimes, the feeling it engendered smacked of shame.

Ulenga didn't know how his American friend lived with the course of action he had chosen, meeting criminals outside the law and fighting on their terms, but it depressed him. Once the raw exhilaration of a fight had had time to fade, Ulenga had to wonder whether he was any better than the men he had defeated. *Murdered,* in the law's eyes, if it ever went to court.

Which, he was confident, it never would.

Whatever happened to him, finally, his future held no trials, no sentencing, no prison cage. The path that he had chosen led to victory or death—and was there really any difference between the two?

Ulenga had the suitcase closed, was fastening its latches, when someone rapped on his door. A muffled voice called out, "Sergeant Ulenga? You are wanted at headquarters."

So.

Taking the pistol with him, Ulenga moved back toward the door.

## 14

Bolan raced across Windhoek, but had to slow and take his time approaching Korrthaan Street in Tauben Glen. Among the thought fragments that filled his mind en route was the idea that Boavida might have used Ulenga's name as bait for Bolan, but it made no difference. The very fact that Boavida *knew* his name was light years beyond ominous.

It meant, for all intents and purposes, that Bolan's comrade had been marked for death.

Only one question remained: Would Bolan be too late?

Bolan drove west on San Nujoma Drive from Windhoek Central, staying on it when the road became C28, then caught the Western Bypass, southbound, to approach Tauben Glen from the west. He wound around by that means onto Ibis Street, then Perihuhn.

His sidetracked thoughts came back into focus as Bolan reached the west end of Korrthaan Street and turned to his right, slowing further for the cruise past Ulenga's apartment house. Bolan had the number, but he didn't need it. It could only be the red house with the Nampol cruisers and the ambulance out front.

On second glance, make that a hearse.

As Bolan passed, two uniformed attendants were emerging from the front door of the red house with a gurney, straining as they cleared the concrete steps, bearing the dead weight of a rubber body bag. The rear doors of the hearse were open, and he saw another bag already lying on the long rear deck inside it. Two down, then, and Bolan obviously couldn't stop to ask if either of them was his friend.

That problem solved itself as Bolan saw a news van, branded with the call sign of a local radio station, turn onto Korrthaan Street from the east. He knew from tuning into the Jetta's radio since he'd arrived that standards for reporting news in Windhoek were about the same as in the States. *If it bleeds, it leads*. And since most of the broadcasts were in English, he would have no trouble following the story when it aired.

How long would that be? With the recent spate of violence, he'd noticed frequent bulletins and "updates," many a regurgitation of the facts and speculation already reported earlier. Another shooting would be on the air as soon as the reporters could compile some basic information and transmit it to the brass at headquarters for broadcasting.

All Bolan had to do was wait.

The hardest job right, despite his ingrained sniper's patience.

Putting Korrthaan Street behind him, knowing that a second pass would give the Nampol uniforms due cause to flag him down, Bolan left Tauben Glen and went to find someplace where he could get a cup of coffee, drink it in his car, listen to the breaking news.

If it was bad…well, by the time he heard the worst confirmed, he would have laid the basic framework for a scheme of shock-and-awe retaliation.

Scorched earth. And no one would be left standing on the other side when Bolan's bloody work was done.

"YES, I UNDERSTAND. Keep me informed of any new developments. This number, yes."

Captain Fanuel Gurirab cradled the telephone receiver, swallowing the urge he felt to smash it into fragments on his desktop. When he saw the tremor in his hand, he was not sure whether it sprang from rage or self-contempt.

Throughout his years of service, he had done things—

many things—that did not make him proud. Some had been done in the pursuit of justice, or at least of vengeance, where the law had proved itself inadequate. Others were done to make his private life more comfortable and to pave the way for his eventual retirement.

Even so, until this moment Gurirab had never been complicit in the murder of another Nampol officer. He could not call Ulenga innocent, since the sergeant was apparently involved in vigilante killings with the foreigner who still remained at large, but always in the past Gurirab had found ways to rationalize his behavior, excuse his transgressions. Prohibition of drugs was a failure, so what did it hurt to ignore the popular traffic, and make a small profit himself? The Mayombe Liberation Front waged war against the Angolan government, not Namibia's. Who really cared if they raised money in Windhoek? Even piracy at sea could be shrugged off. Were not the wealthy shipping companies insured against losses?

But Gurirab knew that he had crossed a line, and there could be no turning back. He did not contemplate confession or surrender to his own superiors, but wondered how long he could live with the oppressive secret of his crime. A lifetime, possibly…but what did that amount to, in the scheme of things?

There would, of course, be an investigation of Ulenga's murder. Gurirab knew he would have a day, or two at most, to polish his report and get the so-called facts in order. As to what he'd say or write about his conversations with Moses Kaujeua, Second Deputy Assistant Minister for Home Affairs, the captain had no clear idea. If he "forgot" that they had spoken, Kaujeua might report it, making Gurirab appear evasive and dishonest. If Gurirab related their discussions, editing the crucial details, Kaujeua might deny them or present a version contradicting Gurirab's and trip him up.

The Nampol brass, of course, would side with his superior.

At least, until they heard Gurirab's tapes.

The captain might be weak, corrupt, even an accomplice

to murder, but no one could say he was stupid. He understood bureaucracy, and ever since his first promotion beyond sergeant, ten years earlier, Gurirab had been documenting the misconduct of his various superiors. Call it insurance—or a pistol pointed at his heart—if anyone found out before he had to play one of his secret cards in self-defense.

Perhaps that time had not arrived. Gurirab would not know for sure for a day or two. While he waited, he would draft two separate reports: one that exonerated both himself and Kaujeua of any wrongdoing, and a second one that cast Kaujeua as a foul conspirator, coercing Gurirab into assisting him. Of course, the fact that Gurirab had taped Kaujeua meant that he—the valiant Nampol captain—planned to topple the corrupt assistant minister from the beginning.

He had simply been too late to save Sergeant Ulenga—who, when all was said and done, had chosen his own fate by turning to a life of crime.

It was a tidy package, anyway he looked at it.

It might just save Gurirab's life—and his career, as well.

THE NEWS FOUND BOLAN sipping mediocre coffee in a parking lot across the street from a convenience store where he had purchased it. He hadn't lingered at the store itself, because a white man lounging in a car, mid morning, was a curious phenomenon that might be stored away in memory. From where he sat, in shade beside a service station that had given up the ghost and sat collecting dust, he had a clear view of the street and no one could creep up behind him without being seen in Bolan's rearview mirror.

Bolan got the word at 10:06 a.m., from an announcer whose tone never varied whether he was reading soccer scores or briefing listeners about mass murder in Sudan. The reader had no names to offer, but he told his audience that a policeman had been killed in Tauben Glen by two or more assailants at his home. One of the gunmen was reported dead, as well, apparently shot by the officer in self-defense. More details were expected to become available…

Bolan switched off the radio, finished his coffee, and picked up the list of targets he'd compiled with Ulenga, his first day in Windhoek. There were still plenty to choose from, but he wanted something that would hit home with the MLF in no uncertain terms.

He thought about the Dragunov stowed in the Jetta's trunk, deciding it was time that he reached out and touched someone.

But who? And where?

Why not the MLF's headquarters on Ompilo Street, in Hakahana? He could take it to the source, and see how Boavida liked it when the war came home to roost.

Of course, simply removing Boavida wouldn't finish Bolan's mission. This appeared to be a case where cutting off the snake's head only meant that it would sprout another, and another after that. The MLF's commanders would be safe, across the border in Angola, where they could appoint an endless string of proxy leaders for their operation in Namibia.

As long as they had soldiers.

And to eliminate the troops, Bolan would need them all together in one place. Not Windhoek, where the collateral damage might be catastrophic. Bolan needed his targets removed to a safe killing ground—safe for innocents, that was. And while he had a spot in mind, ironically, he needed Oscar Boavida to collect his troops.

So, Hakahana it would be, but with a twist.

The suburb's name meant "hurry up" in the Herero language, which was perfect.

Bolan heard the numbers ticking over in his head, and knew that he was running out of time.

"I UNDERSTAND," CAPTAIN Acosta told his agitated caller, frowning as he spoke into the telephone. "Perhaps it would be best if you left Windhoek for the present. To deprive your enemy of targets, eh? A cunning strategy."

"That's all you have to say?" Boavida demanded at the far end of the line.

"What else?" Acosta asked, all innocence. "You've called

to tell me your decision, have you not? And I believe it is a wise one, in the present circumstances."

"But…I thought…" Another silence, as the Angolan struggled to put his thoughts in order, then he asked, "Would it be possible for you to grant me sanctuary?"

*So that's it,* Acosta thought, unable to restrain his smile.

"Unfortunately," he replied, "I am in no position to accommodate you in this matter. As I'm sure you realize, my country values its relationship with SWAPO in Angola."

"Even while you arm the MLF," Boavida said, "to unseat the government?"

"There is no black and white in politics," Acosta said. "You have experience enough to know that, Oscar. Granting you asylum at the embassy, if that's what you're suggesting, could produce a chain reaction of unfortunate events that even I cannot foresee."

"What about Cuba, then?" the MLF commander asked, surprising him.

Acosta sighed. "That raises immigration problems, as I'm sure you recognize," he answered. "If you leave Namibia, perhaps, and then apply for residency from another country. But it would be a matter for our Ministry of Labor and Social Security. Of course, I would be happy to provide endorsement of your application at the proper time."

"I see." The tone of Boavida's voice implied dull resignation. "Have you made arrangements yet with my replacement?" he inquired.

"I don't know what you mean," Acosta told him, honestly.

"Whoever may be next in line," Boavida said, "when I'm dead or driven into exile."

"Oscar, why excite yourself?" Acosta asked, hoping that he had managed to project a soothing tone. "You have a good plan, to escape the city for a time and shelter at your stronghold in the countryside. Hold to it. Take as many of your soldiers with you as you can. Let the authorities clean up whatever mess remains."

"You know of the policeman?" Boavida asked him, sharply, making no attempt to cover the suspicion in his voice.

"I have my sources," Acosta said. "I would be of no use to you if I did not."

Boavida made a sound that could have been a simple throat-clearing, or possibly a sneer of rude contempt. Acosta opted to ignore it, waiting for the paranoid Angolan to say more or terminate the call.

"I can expect no further help, then?" Boavida asked, at last.

"No further help?" Acosta echoed down the line. "Oscar, you've had no end of help since your arrival in Namibia, including both financial and material support, if you recall. I hope that when this crisis is behind us, our relationship remains intact. However, it's unfair of you, I must say, to expect that I should actually fight your battles for you in the streets."

Boavida muttered something—maybe Portuguese, probably a curse of some kind—and the line went dead. Acosta gently cradled the receiver of his telephone and rocked back in his swivel chair. People said Latins were excitable, but Africans, in his experience, tended to be explosive. That was good for revolution—good for business, too—but it made working with their warlords a royal *dolor en el culo*.

A pain in the ass.

Feeling that pain presently, Acosta wondered if a stiff shot of rum would be helpful.

And answered himself as expected—*why not?*

HAKAHANA LIES NORTH OF Windhoek proper, between the suburbs of Big Bend and Okuryangava. Ompilo Street runs north-south between Ehonga to Etetwe, lined with various commercial buildings in assorted sizes. The Mayombe Liberation Front's headquarters was located near the south end of Ompilo, near its intersection with Edimba Street. Even here, so close to Windhoek, pavement seemed to be a problem. While Omuve Street, one block west of Ompilo, had been paved with asphalt, those to the east and west of it had not.

Bolan cared nothing for the surface underneath the Jetta's

tires, as he went looking for a sniper's nest. He found it cat-ercornered from the MLF facility, a square three-story block of shops with offices upstairs. Its flat roof would provide the view he needed. All he had to do was climb up there, without encountering civilians on the way, and pick his shot.

Simple? Not quite.

A white man carrying a duffel bag that measured four feet long to fit the Russian sniper rifle zipped inside, climbing a service ladder to the rooftop of the building he'd selected, could expect to sound alarms with any local he met along the way. Even with its stock folded, the Dragunov SVDS still measured 44.7 inches from muzzle to pistol grip, and weighed nearly ten pounds without its scope or loaded magazine.

Bolan relaxed a little when he reached the rooftop without incident and found himself alone up there. Crossing the roof to reach the building's southwest corner, he sat down, opened his bag, and set about his final preparation of the Dragunov. First step: unfold the 12.6-inch stock. Next step: retrieve a ten-round double-stacked box magazine and slot it into the rifle's receiver. Third: attach a foot-long silencer over the weapon's slotted flash suppressor.

Last, but certainly not least, Bolan removed the PSO-1 tele-scopic sight—short for *Pritsel Snaipersky Optichesky,* "optical sniper sight" in Russian—from its separate carrying case and attached it to his weapon with the proprietary quick-release mounting bracket. That done, he used the sight to peer across Ompilo Street and find his target.

Soldiers were hustling around MLF headquarters, loading bags and boxes into SUVs out front and in a parking lot behind the building. Bolan watched them, realizing that he'd barely made it in the nick of time as they cleaned out the place, pre-paring to evacuate. He had a fair idea of where they would be going, thanks to Ulenga's briefing at the onset of their short campaign, and Bolan hoped to send them off in style. Not leaderless—at least, not yet—but in a hell-for-leather hurry that would ramp up their anxiety and keep it off the chart.

Five minutes after setting up his vigil, Bolan spotted Boavida exiting the building through the rear. Soldiers surrounded him, weapons barely concealed as they escorted the man to a waiting Land Rover. Bolan scoped in the hustling group and fixed his crosshairs on a skull immediately to the left of Boavida's, and zeroed on the flesh just visible behind a small pierced ear.

He squeezed the rifle's trigger, then swung at once to Boavida's right without assessing his first shot, and fired again. Five coughing noises from the Russian piece, in all, and Boavida stood alone, cringing without a bit of cover in the parking lot, bodies and blood strewn everywhere around his feet.

When Boavida began to scream, Bolan retreated from the roof's edge, swiftly breaking down his weapon, stowing it away. If his luck held, and he could make it to the Jetta without meeting any obstacles, he could begin the drive to Boavida's hideaway.

A ghost town in the desert.

And when the Executioner was finished, it would have a few more ghosts in residence.

"HOW DID HE MISS ME? How? The others…all dead! Did you see them?"

Boavida knew that he was babbling, but he could not seem to stop. Even as one of his soldiers wiped the cooling blood and gray matter from Boavida's cheek with a large handkerchief, the MLF's commander could not hold his tongue.

"To kill five men around me… How could I survive?"

"Maybe he only had five bullets in the magazine," one of his bodyguards suggested.

"Do you think so?" Boavida asked him.

Which provoked a shrug. "It's possible," the soldier said. "Some rifles only hold five rounds."

"The bodies," Boavida said, then stopped himself. There'd been no time for moving corpses when he'd fled, much less concealing them effectively. Police would find the dead men where he'd left them and begin to search for him, as well. His luck was running out in Windhoek. Bribes could only stretch so far.

But they would not find him in Kolmanskop.

His choice of an emergency retreat had been inspired, if Boavida did say so himself. Not only isolated and abandoned in the southern Namib Desert, but reputed to be overrun with ghosts of former residents—black miners who'd been overworked and underpaid by German masters for a grim half century until the diamond fields played out. The unmarked graves of hundreds had been left behind, forgotten and reclaimed by shifting sands.

Namibians steered clear of Kolmanskop, encouraged to avoid it during recent years by Boavida's men, who spread rumors of hauntings through the rural villages and made sure any trespassers were never seen again. It should be simple to hide out there, waiting for the storm in Windhoek to subside.

And after that?

Clearly, it would be necessary to repair some ties with the Namibian officials who had managed to ignore the MLF before the recent troubles started. With journalists involved and asking questions, it would be more difficult for Boavida and his men to operate in anything approximating secrecy. More difficult, but not impossible perhaps.

At least, if he was not abandoned by his allies in the government.

Money would be required to soothe them, certainly. And Boavida might be forced to scale back operations temporarily to keep a low profile. He could do that, make all required assurances and follow through on them, if given half a chance.

But all of that demanded that he stay alive.

And any hope of that, right now, lay in the desert.

At the ghost town known as Kolmanskop.

**15**

In its heyday, Kolmanskop—Afrikaans for Coleman's Hill, named for a nineteenth-century teamster who lost his ox and wagon on the site during one of the Namib Desert's hellacious sand storms—rivaled any boom town of the old American West. Built in the style of a traditional German village, it included a school and a ballroom, a theater and sporting hall, a casino and bowling alley, an ice factory, electric power plant and a hospital with the first X-ray station in the southern hemisphere. Africa's first tramcars carried shoppers through the streets of Kolmanskop, while a rail line hauled its diamonds six miles westward to the seaport of Lüderitz.

All gone? Not quite.

Though Kolmanskop's last human residents bailed out in 1954, the desert's arid climate has preserved their former lodgings and amenities. Windows devoid of glass admit the searing wind, and rooms have been carpeted in sand, knee-deep in some buildings, and the paint has been sandblasted from the walls.

But uninhabited? Not even close.

Despite its desolation, the Namib—like all of Earth's great deserts—teems with life. Reptiles abound, including dune lizards that survive on scorching sand by keeping two feet elevated at all times. Barking geckos utter a nocturnal call that mimics an elusive bird. Twenty species of snakes call the desert home, thirteen of them venomous. Mammals also survive in the dunes, ranging in size from mice and rats to jackals and the pony-size gemsbok, a spiral-horned antelope. Scuttling through the vacant homes and shops of Kolmanskop beside the rats are scorpions, beetles and baboon spiders the size of your hand.

Regardless of the climate, there is no eradicating life—or death.

Bolan had driven south from Windhoek on the B1 highway to Keetmanshoop, then west from there on the B4 to Lüderitz. In Lüderitz he'd swapped the Jetta for a Nissan Xterra N50. The road to Kolmanskop from Lüderitz was clear, at least in theory, but he would be leaving it for navigation on the dunes, hence the requirement for a vehicle with four-wheel drive. The Xterra compact SUV could handle anything he might encounter in the Namib, short of sinkholes that could swallow semi-trailers, drowning them—and any human passengers—in tons of shifting sand.

The sun was setting by the time Bolan had finished packing his gear in the Nissan. After a quick meal at a German buffet on Hafen Street, overlooking the harbor, he was on the road again. He'd wanted Boavida's caravan to reach the ghost town first and settle in before he showed up to disrupt their evening.

Half a mile from Lüderitz he killed his high beams, navigating through the moonless night with aid from his night-vision goggles. Bolan also kept the dashboard lights turned low, with only enough illumination to allow reading of the Nissan's odometer. He watched for the sign that marked his turnoff for the access road to Kolmanskop and followed it for half a mile, then went off-road with the Xterra.

Bolan wondered how many adversaries waited for him in the ghost town up ahead. He would find out when he got there and had come to grips with them. Until then, speculation was a waste of time and energy. He took for granted that they'd be expecting trouble, but they couldn't know the form that it would take, or when it would arrive. None of them knew that they were dealing with the Executioner.

And by the time they found out, it would be too late.

BOAVIDA PACED AROUND the lobby of an inn that had once
housed guests and served fine meals to residents of Kolmanskop. Although the floor had been swept clear, as far as possible, sand still crunched underneath his boots with every step.
A gecko watched him from the northeast corner of the ceiling,
hanging upside-down with toes like suction cups, apparently
bemused by obsessive movements of the khaki-clad intruder
on its normal hunting ground.

It had been years since Boavida had personally fired a
weapon, but he wore an AK-47 slung over his shoulder like a
soldier at the battlefront—which was exactly how he felt this
night. Hounded from Windhoek by an enemy he'd never met,
spattered with blood and brains as bullets dropped his bodyguards within arm's reach of Boavida, he felt cornered, driven
to distraction in his desert exile.

Would the enemy pursue him there? Did he have knowledge of the hideaway that Boavida had prepared soon after
coming to Namibia?

A part of Boavida's mind hope that the bastard *would* come.
Let him walk into the trap that Boavida had prepared for him
and meet his death where so many had died before, away from
prying eyes. Perhaps he could be captured and interrogated,
grilled for information, then dissected for the amusement of
the men whose friends he'd killed over the past day and a half.

If Boavida found out who had sent him, who'd unleashed
this plague of torment, then what? He could always find an address, send the hunter's ears or other parts of him back to his
masters as a souvenir. Teach them the folly of intruding where
they were not wanted. Where they had no place as westerners.

The CIA had learned that lesson over time, grudgingly,
during the long war in Angola, but it seemed that someone
in authority had not absorbed the message. Africa was different. It had devoured European armies in the past, and could
again, if necessary. Solitary meddlers might succeed in the
short term, but they could not subdue the continent. Its native
people would prevail, outlasting any white men who were sent
against them, from whatever source.

But, then, why did the fear keep Boavida pacing restlessly by lamplight? Why was he unable to sit still and rest?

Because he was not Africa. In truth, as Boavida knew too well, he did not represent the best inhabitants of that dynamic continent. He'd been a warrior once, and proud of it, but times had changed. He was an officer these days, which meant directing others, letting them do all the fighting, while he sat behind a desk and issued orders.

Boavida had grown soft in his position of security, behind the lines.

And soft men frightened easily.

The best way to regain his strength and the respect of those who served him was to get his hands bloody again. To prove that he was not a coward, but a soldier who could kill without remorse and glory in it.

Possibly, this night, he'd have that chance.

Redemption could be his.

And still he trembled, pacing while the lizard watched him from above, wearing its mirthless smile.

"AND THE SNIPER FIRED FROM…over there?" Captain Gurirab asked, turning to stare across Ompilo Street.

"Yes, sir," the burly sergeant answered. "Five casings recovered from the rooftop. Five kills over here."

They stood together in the parking lot behind the building leased by the Mayombe Liberation Front as a headquarters for its so-called philanthropical activities. Large bloodstains baked in abstract patterns on the pavement at their feet.

"It still surprises me," Gurirab said.

"What does, sir?" the sergeant asked.

"So much blood inside one person."

"Ah. Yes, sir."

"We're dealing with a marksman now," Gurirab said. "The other cases, it was all machine guns and explosives. This one, if he's not the same one, hits his target five times out of five at…what? A hundred yards?"

"About that, sir."

"It wouldn't be a challenge with a stationary target, granted. But with five men moving—rapidly, we may assume—it adds a new level of complexity."

"Yes, sir."

"And none of them was Boavida?" Gurirab asked, for the second time since he'd arrived on site.

"No, sir, unless their immigration cards were forged."

*Too bad,* the captain thought. *That might have ended it.* He said, "No, I suspect their papers are in order. Boavida doesn't fool with dicey paperwork. His crimes are of a grander nature."

"Yet we don't arrest him," the sergeant observed, his tone cautiously neutral.

"It prompts curiosity, eh?"

Gurirab thought of Sergeant Ulenga, asked himself if the man who stood before him was also seething at frustration over favors done for certain violators of the law. How many Nampol officers already felt the same?

"You've searched the building?" Gurirab inquired.

"No, sir. We're waiting for a warrant."

"Never mind that. It's a murder scene. For all we know, the killer may be hiding in there at this very moment, Sergeant."

"Sir? He fired from over— Ah, I see. Of course, you're right, sir. We'll begin the search at once."

The sergeant hustled off to follow his instructions, leaving Gurirab alone with remnants of the dead. Their blood on blacktop, and the crude chalk marks outlining where they'd fallen after someone with a decent rifle and a better eye had blown the brains out of their skulls. Five head shots at a hundred yards in rapid semiauto fire took practice and experience.

If he was still up there...

A sudden chill gripped Captain Gurirab, despite the sun that did its best to bake him in his wilted uniform. There was no sniper on the rooftop presently, of course.

Where had he gone?

Perhaps to finish what he'd started with the MLF. Stalking

his targets to wherever they had gone, believing they could either hide from him or lure him in and kill him.

Kolmanskop? Why not?

Captain Gurirab had a choice to make. He could stand back, let nature take its course, and see which way the bureaucratic wind blew when the gunsmoke cleared away. Or he could lead a troop of officers to Kolmanskop and try to intervene. Which could mean clashing with the MLF commandos Boavida would have gathered to protect him from his unknown nemesis.

Gurirab had the blood of Ulenga on his hands already. Should he risk more men without consulting his superiors? And if he sought direction, how would they respond?

He knew what a policeman dedicated to the law would do, but he had slipped so far beyond the pale, that knowledge did not make his grim decision any easier.

Five minutes later, cursing bitterly, the captain opened his cell phone.

CAPTAIN RODRIGO ACOSTA lit his third cigar of the day, sitting in his comfortable leather chair, his feet propped on a corner of his desk. Life at the Cuban Embassy was good, all things considered, but he wondered if it was coming to an end for him.

The worst thing that a diplomat could do, short of provoking war without approval of superiors, was to embarrass his homeland. The same was doubly true for consular officials like Acosta, who were actually covert operatives pledged to keep their covert actions secret, running smoothly, without any of the difficulties known as "blowback" to his counterparts from the United States.

Acosta's illegal support for the Mayombe Liberation Front had been approved by all the relevant officials in Havana, and he had received cooperation from the men who mattered most in Windhoek. However, with everything seemingly about to blow up in his face, Acosta had no doubt who would receive the lion's share of blame for any headlines about Cuban spying and subversion—or for any shock waves that disrupted Cuban dealings with Angola.

Certainly, it would be *his* head on the chopping block. And while the scandal might not mean the end of life itself, as would have been the case in days gone by, it would undoubtedly spell doom for his career. If scapegoats were required, Acosta would be first to feel the heat—and hear his sentence read in court.

Acosta was aware of the conditions found in Cuban prisons—Mango Jobo, El Sinfín, Sandino and the rest—and he had no intention of becoming one more starving scarecrow in a cage. Defection would be preferable, as would suicide. But thankfully, if the Namibian assignment blew up in his face, he had a third alternative available.

Spies, by definition, deal with shady people every day. They are involved in criminal activity, either supporting or opposing it, and frequently enjoy an opportunity to profit from those illegitimate transactions. Some focused on duty and denied themselves that chance. Captain Acosta, on the other hand, had never seen any reason why he should not mix business and pleasure.

At the present time, he had anonymous accounts at banks in the Bahamas and the Cayman Islands, one in Liechtenstein and one in Switzerland. Who could predict where fate might lead him in the years to come? He also had an emergency bankroll concealed in the floor safe beneath his desk, with passports in two different names. One Cuban and one Argentinean, just for variety.

Acosta was ready to go at a moment's notice—but would it be necessary?

There was at least a chance, he thought, that his potential problem would resolve itself. So far, Boavida and his men had proved inept at dealing with their enemies. Their only victory so far was killing a policeman whom they'd trapped at home, after a source inside his own department had supplied his name and address. Left to do it by themselves, Acosta thought they'd still be flailing aimlessly and losing more men by the hour—as, in fact, they had outside their own headquarters, after Boavida made his plan to flee Windhoek.

And if the enemy who still survived should find them there? If he should wipe them out entirely, who would then be left to spill the details of Acosta's dealings with the MLF?

No one.

Smiling, the hopeful Cuban let himself relax and savor his cigar.

WALKING THROUGH THE DUNES of the Numib Desert, all green before the LUCIE night-vision goggles he wore, Bolan was reminded of his first strike in Namibia, against the pirates at Durissa Bay. There was no river here to guide him, but he had a compass and his GPS device to keep him well on course. The goggles penetrated shadows and dispensed with any risk of stepping on a cobra or viper in the darkness.

Even so, the warrior took his time. Rushing to Kolmanskop accomplished nothing, since the MLF had found the ghost town months ago, according to Ulenga. More than ample time to rig defenses for a last-ditch stand, and Bolan would gain nothing through a swift approach that led to him blundering into a trap. Better to scout the unfamiliar ground while his intended prey relaxed, feeling secure in safety, relaxing their guard somewhat. When he was ready, and he sensed that Boavida's men were not, then he would make his move.

As far as Bolan knew, he had all night.

And that would be a lifetime for his enemies.

There was a chance, of course, that someone in officialdom would try to help the MLF with reinforcements. That idea assumed that other Nampol officers or military personnel knew the location of his fallback hardsite in the desert. If they did, and if they chose to help him, Bolan might be forced to cut and run. In the Namib, he'd be exposed, an easy target if they came in helicopters or in dune buggies. And if they were police-protected, he would have to abandon his plan because of his private vow against the use of deadly force on cops.

No part of that scenario encouraged him to rush headlong

against his adversaries. Bolan was adaptable in combat situations—proof of that being the fact that he was still alive—but he had never changed a plan because of fear that something *might* occur. If the police or army showed up, he would deal with it by means he deemed appropriate. Until then, he was sticking with plan A.

Another half mile to the ghost town where his enemies were waiting for a date with Death.

THE WIND WAS PICKING UP, a constant feature of the open desert, shifting sand so that the landscape sometimes changed dramatically between dusk and dawn. Large moths had blown in through the open windows of the inn where Boavida had his quarters, fluttering around his lamp, casting their giant spastic shadows on the walls and ceiling.

*Ghosts,* he thought, and barked a note of hollow laughter. He'd been raised by parents mired in superstition, who believed the spirits of their ancestors were constantly on watch around them, while a shadow world of demons waited for an opening, a chance to rob them of their souls. That thought had terrified him as a child, until he came to realize that all the demons found on Earth were human beings, capable of any vile atrocity without the goading of an insubstantial wraith.

Still, waiting in the ruins of the ghost town for some word from Windhoek, hoping to be told his enemies had all been found and executed, Boavida felt some of the dread from childhood creeping back. The darkness and the atmosphere of the deserted settlement almost convinced him that a doorway could be found between the world he understood and mad realms of the supernatural, where ghastly things lay waiting for a chance to strike at mortal men.

"Ridiculous," he said aloud, forgetting that there was a guard on station in the room, within earshot. Turning, embarrassed, Boavida silenced any questions with a glare, waiting until the guard's eyes were averted to resume his restless pacing.

*He thinks I'm crazy,* Boavida thought. And would the

soldier necessarily be wrong? Pacing and talking to himself might be interpreted as symptoms of a mental breakdown, all the more so under pressure such as Boavida had experienced of late. Who could dispute his right to lose touch with reality?

That almost made him laugh, but Boavida swallowed it, refusing to provide his bodyguard with any further evidence of lunacy. The very last thing that he needed, while holed up in Kolmanskop, a fugitive, was for his men to lose whatever dwindling vestige of respect for him they still retained by spreading rumors that he'd gone insane.

And what must his superiors be thinking in Cuanza Norte Province in Angola? Had they already decided that promoting him was a mistake? Were plans in motion to relieve him, drag him home for trial by court-martial, perhaps for execution by a firing squad? If so, could Boavida possibly do anything to head off that result?

A victory at Kolmanskop, the absolute destruction of his enemies, might help if it was not too late. Proving that he could rebound from the worst adversity might demonstrate the wisdom of allowing Boavida to retain command and carry on with operations in Namibia.

Or it might simply demonstrate that he had done too little, far too late.

In any case, his last, best hope lay here, among the sand dunes and deserted buildings. He could not return to Windhoek—much less to Angola—without managing at least one victory. If he could only salvage something from the ruins that surrounded him—

The *crump* of an explosion echoed through the ghost town, making Boavida flinch. He turned to face his watchman, found the soldier standing rigid, torn between an impulse to investigate and his sworn duty to remain on station.

"Go!" Boavida snapped, as he slipped his AK-47 off its shoulder sling. "I'm right behind you."

**16**

Once Bolan had confirmed the presence of his enemies in Kolmanskop, he moved to close the door on any possible escape. Scouting the fringes of the ghost town and its dunes, he counted thirteen vehicles, all SUVs with four wheel-drive except for one small off-road motorcycle. Doing the math, he guessed that five men could ride comfortably in an SUV, or they could squeeze a couple more behind the backseat, in the cargo area. Sixty guns for sure, with one or two more on the bike, with a max of eighty, eighty-five.

Still doable, if Bolan watched his step and took advantage of the desert night.

Vehicles first. The bandoleer he wore across his chest held twenty VOG-25P caseless rounds, with one already chambered. Bolan's problem was that Boavida's soldiers had not parked their rides together in the semblance of a standard motor pool. Five clustered near what might have been an old hotel, four stood outside the ghost town's former railroad station at the other end of town, the rest were scattered in between, parked close to buildings where, he guessed, their occupants had gone to ground. The bike was on its kickstand, tucked away between two long-abandoned stores.

Lights shone from windows of the buildings where the vehicles were parked, but they were clearly cast by lamps of some kind, either burning fuel or run from batteries. The sole exception was the building Bolan took for a hotel or inn. The light in one of its front windows flickered, as if generated by an open fire.

The lights were helpful—and potentially deceptive. Just because some buildings were illuminated, Bolan could not take for granted that the others were unoccupied. It would be smart to station shooters in the blacked-out shops and homes, waiting and watching for a target to reveal itself. Someone creeps in and goes to snipe an easy mark through lighted windows, getting cocky, and he's dead before he knows it.

Maybe.

On the other hand, the men he'd come to kill might just be frightened of the dark.

Bolan decided he would hit the cars parked at the railroad station first, see who—if anyone—emerged, and find out how it played from there. The GP-30 gave him reach to hang back from the blast zone, covered by the darkness while he gauged the MLF's reaction to an uninvited visitor.

Round one away. It struck the tailgate of a Range Rover Rhino and sent out a shock wave to rouse any sleepers in town. The car stood on its nose, riding fire to a vertical plane, then crashed back to the ground with tires sizzling and melting. It spewed enough fuel to ignite the Toyota 4Runner beside it and saved Bolan one round that way. The second car blew just as Bolan squeezed off with his sights fixed on a Honda Element.

The third explosion brought men spilling from the one-time railroad station, but they couldn't spot him in the dark without a muzzle-flash to give him up. The GP-30 offered none to speak of, with the nitrocellulose propellant built into its caseless rounds, so Bolan let it do his talking for him, left Boavida's men milling in the firelight as he fired his third grenade at the remaining SUV.

It was a Chevrolet Captiva that would have been fun driving on the dunes before it turned into a raging fireball, hurling plumes of burning gasoline like blasts from a flamethrower toward the shooters gathered on the railway station's platform. One of them got roasted where he stood, a jiggling human torch, while his companions ran for cover anywhere that they could find it.

Fair enough. Game on.

FLYING SOUTH FROM WINDHOEK in the HAL Light Observation Helicopter he had managed to secure from Nampol's tiny air wing, Captain Fanuel Gurirab felt as if he was rushing toward a funeral, perhaps his own. If that turned out to be the case, he was prepared to pay the price, redeem some vestige of his honor if it was not already too late.

Five well-armed officers accompanied him, together with the helicopter's two crew members who were also Nampol sergeants. Twenty more were converging on Kolmanskop by land from various rural stations, but he had no patience for the long drive south. It seemed to Gurirab that he had wasted too much time already, possibly his whole career, and he refused to spend another futile moment idling in complacency.

Their whirlybird was manufactured by Hindustan Aeronautics Limited of Bangalore, India, with a cruising speed of 161 miles per hour and a service ceiling of 21,300 feet. On this night, they were flying much lower than that, barely a thousand feet above the Namib Desert's undulating sand dunes, buoyed by the latent heat still radiating from the vast ocean of sunbaked sand.

They were a hundred miles or so from Kolmanskop, but Captain Gurirab had spent the whole flight worrying about what he would do when they arrived. It was impossible for him to know how Boavida's gunmen would react to the arrival of a helicopter with the word Police emblazoned on its fuselage. They might think that the officers were sent as reinforcements, based on prior collaboration with Nampol, or they might fear arrest and open fire on sight, blasting the chopper from the sky.

With that in mind, Gurirab had ordered his pilots to set down a quarter-mile short of the ghost town. He and his men could hike in from the landing zone—not truly a surprise,

given the helicopter's lights and noise, but still better than
being shot like birds over a hunter's blind.

This way, at least, they had a chance of getting into Kolmanskop alive.

And then what?

Gurirab would see how they were greeted, how close he
could get to Boavida without gunfire. If he could arrest the
man in charge, even use Boavida as a hostage, then the situation might be saved. If not…well, they would have to fight
their way in, find whatever cover was available at Kolmanskop, and hold on while they waited for the other Nampol officers to finally arrive.

The darkness yawned before Fanuel Gurirab as he hurtled
southward, like the maw of some huge monster poised to swallow him alive. The captain wondered whether he would see
another sunrise, for the first time in his life uncertain that it
mattered either way.

BOAVIDA FELT AS IF HE WERE trapped in a recurring nightmare.
Only hours earlier, he had been spattered with the blood and
brains of men sworn to defend him, cringing with their bodies
at his feet and waiting for a bullet to snuff out his own life. He
had survived that ordeal somehow, suffered the humiliation of
a flight into the wilderness, and yet seemed his enemies had
found him once again, bringing Hell to his very doorstep.

As he lurched out of the former inn, clutching his AK-47
like a holy talisman before him, Boavida saw three of his
party's vehicles in flames outside the long-abandoned railway
station. Even as he reached the porch, second blast rocked Kolmanskop, tearing another of their SUVs apart and leaving it
a fiery wreck. One of his soldiers, also burning, leaped and
shrieked until another hurled him to the ground and rolled him
in the sand to smother the engulfing fire.

"Go back inside, sir," one of Boavida's watchers cautioned
him. "We don't know where they are."

"Then *find* them!" Boavida bellowed in reply, and wondered even as he spoke how many enemies had trailed him to the ghost town.

Only one had been observed by the survivors at Durissa Bay. In Windhoek there were two, but one of those—the vigilante Nampol officer—had been eliminated. That left one by Boavida's count, unless the white man everyone assumed to be American had found more allies to assist him.

Boavida's mind was reeling as he reached the inn's threshold, ducked in and slammed the door behind him, locking out the night. As if a simple dead bolt lock would keep the man who hunted him from entering and finishing his work.

*He could have killed me back in Windhoek,* Boavida thought. *Why didn't he?*

Was it some kind of strange, sadistic game? Was Boavida meant to suffer hours of anguish first, before he died?

If so, the bastard who'd been sent for him was in for a surprise. Whatever he and his employers might suppose, one did not rise to a commander's rank in the Mayombe Liberation Front by being squeamish or retreating from a fight. Perhaps his rank and its administrative tasks had softened Boavida, but beneath it all he still remained the soldier who had lived in jungle squalor, ambushed government patrols and terrorized opponents in the name of liberty.

And he would not be trapped inside a crumbling guesthouse while his men lay down their lives defending him. It shamed him, and the only way to rinse that shame away was with the blood of his opponent.

Boavida turned back to the door, unlocked it, trying to ignore the trembling in his hand as he unlatched the dead bolt. Once the door was open, he had to force himself to take the next step, as another thunderous explosion almost drove him back inside. He turned in the direction of the latest blast and saw another, closer SUV settle on wings of fire after its fuel tank blew.

Cursing himself to keep his feet in motion, Boavida went in search of his enemies.

BOLAN HAD WORKED HIS way through half of Boavida's vehicles before one of the MLF defenders spotted him. He knew it had to happen, but he was disappointed that he couldn't trash a few more of their rides before the fight was joined in earnest.

As it was, the shooter nearly stumbled over him by accident, coming around a corner of the one-time theater, clumsily grappling with his rifle and his zipper at the same time. Literally caught with his pants down, Bolan decided, as their eyes met and the startled gunman suddenly forgot about his fly. Survival took priority over embarrassment, both hands fumbling to level his Kalashnikov, but he was already too late.

Bolan's three-round burst found the ten-ring and dumped his target over backward, sand spraying from boot heels as they rose into the air. The dead man never got a shot off, but he didn't need to as the stutter of the rounds that killed him echoed through the darkened streets of Kolmanskop.

Not waiting to discover whether anyone had glimpsed the muzzle-flash, Bolan kept moving, feeding the GP-30 another caseless round as he ran. Shouted questions in the dark told him his enemies were still confused, unfocused and, he hoped to keep them chasing shadows for at least a short while longer. And to that end…

Bolan saw the old hotel or inn a hundred yards in front of him, dropped to one knee, and sighted through his LUCIE goggles at the clutch of SUVs parked out in front of it. He sent the VOG round off to do its deadly work. A second was loaded, fired and airborne by the time the first made impact on the windshield of a Great Wall Haval H3 and peeled its roof back with an echo that stung Bolan's ears.

The second HE projectile struck the left-rear door of an Infiniti QX56 and punched through it, flushing the luxury SUV's interior with flames, leaving the body bent and twisted like a beer can crumpled in a biker's fist. Somehow, one of the hubcaps chose that moment to go sailing through the night, a glinting UFO that vanished when it flew beyond the reach of firelight.

As before, the fuel spewing from ruptured tanks helped to

ignite the other vehicles and saved Bolan the effort of destroying each in turn himself. The central street of Kolmanskop
was filled with running, dodging figures, some of them firing
short bursts into shadows at suspected enemies, but none
coming close to Bolan yet.

He took a chance, sighting on one, and dropped him with
a double-tap from thirty yards. Another ran across his line
of fire and joined the other in a dusty wallow, ending face-
up toward the desert sky, sand in his sightless eyes. A third
veered toward the fallen pair, then reconsidered, spinning off
to flee, his mad dash terminated by a 7.62x39 mm round between his shoulder blades.

Then someone spotted him. But Bolan was prepared for it,
already up and running when the shout was raised and soldiers
swung their weapons toward him, firing well before they had
a target sighted. Bullets swarmed around the Executioner like
fat mosquitoes thirsty for his blood, as he dived into cover at
the southeast corner of the long-deserted inn.

OSCAR BOAVIDA SAW THE enemy, or thought he did—a
shadow-shape running along the rim of firelight toward the
inn where Boavida had been hiding moments earlier. He
raised his AK-47 for a shot, then lost the figure as he was
about to squeeze the trigger.

*Damn it!*

He had a choice to make without delay: collect his men and
seek the prowler, or save the time that would be lost and do the
job himself. A leader would not hesitate, and yet...

A surge of self-contempt made the decision for him. Boavida started forward, picking up his pace after a few strides,
making it a chase. He would feel foolish if he found himself
pursuing one of his own soldiers, but the clothes and gear
seemed wrong, as had the shadow-figure's stature, profile, all
of it.

He had a chance to be a hero. One shot, one moment, could
redeem him in the eyes of his subordinates, perhaps even with
his superiors. It would not cancel out the losses suffered by

the MLF over the past two days, but at the very least it would prove he was no coward, cringing in a bunker while his men took all the risks.

A line of footprints in the sand led Boavida from the southwest corner of the inn, where there was light enough to see by, into darkness at the rear. He slowed his pace, cursing the drifts beneath his feet that would not let him move in perfect silence. His ears strained for a corresponding sound, to indicate his target was still running, and heard nothing but the crack of weapons firing aimlessly on Kolmanskop's main street.

The damned fools would be lucky if they didn't kill each other. Meanwhile—

Wait! There *was* another sound, but it was coming from behind him. Not the sound of footsteps, but of…what? Something approaching from a distance, to the north, and closing rapidly. He stopped dead in his tracks until he'd worked it out.

A helicopter.

Boavida knew the MLF had no aircraft, not in Angola or Namibia. Therefore, a helicopter could not be good news— unless, perhaps…

Was it possible that someone in Windhoek would send him aid at Kolmanskop? Nampol, perhaps…or even the elusive Cubans? Even if the helicopter only used its searchlight to pick out their enemy and mark him for elimination, it would be a help.

But if the law had turned against them, Boavida reckoned they were finished.

Should he keep on searching for the shadow-shape he'd briefly glimpsed, or go to meet the aircraft and be done with it, whatever *it* might be? Another tough decision, but he made it, turning back in the direction of the nearing engine sounds.

And found the man whom he'd been seeking, standing right in front of him. Something about his face was strange, *deformed,* as if—

Night-vision goggles!

Boavida understood, began to raise his AK-47, but the silent figure got there first. His weapon hammered Boavida backward into darkness deeper than the desert night, and silent, where he didn't have to think about the helicopter or his reputation any more. Nothing but pain, and in another instant, even that was gone.

THE HELICOPTER'S NOISE told Bolan he was out of time. Whether the new arrivals were coming for him, or planned on mopping up the remnants of the MLF, they would be lawmen. He could wreak more havoc on the rebels as he left, but Bolan's top priority, with Oscar Boavida dead, was getting out of range before he had to deal with any cops.

The fires would draw the chopper into Kolmanskop. If he was quick enough, Bolan imagined he could put some ground between himself and the approaching force, leave them to deal with Boavida's remnants in whatever way they chose, while he backtracked to where he'd left his Nissan SUV.

But walking out, he realized, would take too long.

He'd blown up more than half the vehicles in Kolmanskop, but that still left three SUVs and one dirt bike to choose from—if he found one with the keys in place. And if Boavida's men weren't fleeing at that very moment themselves, from the airborne new arrivals.

Bolan wasted no more time considering his options. He could see the chopper's running lights as he dodged soldiers on the move, circling beyond the reach of firelight toward an SUV that sat alone, outside the empty hulk of Kolmanskop's one-time casino. Peering through the driver's window, he could see the dangling key fob. No need for security on that score, he supposed, when you were camped out in a ghost town in the middle of the planet's oldest desert. Who would steal your car?

Except, perhaps, a passing Executioner.

The dome light made him wince briefly, but it switched off when he closed the driver's door. A second later he was rolling without headlights, but he couldn't kill the daytime running lamps that are a standard feature on most modern cars, worried they might attract the chopper for a strafing run, hoping the fires and random muzzle-flashes visible from Kolmanskop might cover him.

When he had almost reached the ghost town's outskirts, one of Boavida's soldiers ran in front of Bolan, as if trying to obstruct his passage with a body-block. It was no contest, flesh and bone against the hurtling machine, with power, weight and grim determination all on Bolan's side. He felt the first impact, and then the lurch of running over something, cushioned by a drift of sand cradling the broken man.

Then he was out and off across the dunes, craning his neck to watch the helicopter as it approached. He couldn't see its occupants, but watched the whirlybird pursue its course toward Kolmanskop without veering away to intercept him. In another moment he was past it, saw its shape receding in his rearview mirror as a spotlight flared, probing ahead toward Kolmanskop.

*Good hunting,* Bolan thought, and kept the pedal to the medal.

All he had to think about, from that point on, was getting back to Windhoek, past whatever land patrols might be in play, and making contact with a charter pilot who would carry him across the border.

Once he'd done a final bit of cleaning up.

# Epilogue

*Christ Church, Fidel Castro Street, Windhoek*

Captain Rodrigo Acosta liked to think that he possessed as fine a sense of irony as any man, but he did not appreciate the humor of the site selected by Moses Kaujeua for their meeting. As a Cuban spy, Acosta might have been expected to admire the street's name, but the Second Deputy Assistant Minister for Home Affairs should certainly have known that agents of the Castro revolution found no solace at a church.

Acosta stood outside the looming structure, opened to the public—or at least the Lutheran portion of it—in October 1910. Across the street, a giant rifleman on horseback, cast from bronze, studied Acosta from his place outside Windhoek's Old Fort. The Rider Memorial, erected in 1912, symbolized white conquest of the land and Namibia's aboriginal people, thus posing another insult to Acosta and all that he'd believed since he was educated by the state in childhood.

And Kaujeua was late. Ten minutes and counting, despite the urgency of his assistant's call requesting—no, *demanding*—that Acosta meet him for an urgent conversation in this public place, where they could not be overheard. The politician's tardiness was aggravating. It would be a challenge for Acosta to be civil, never mind accommodating. Indeed, he saw no need for any further meetings, since their problem had been solved last night.

A bloodbath in the desert, and the slate was clean. There

would be no more bungling on the part of Boavida. He was on his way to fill an unmarked pauper's grave. The men who'd died along with him were revolutionary soldiers, but the world was full of cannon fodder. Those who fell were easily replaced.

At last, Acosta saw Kaujeua's car approaching. Naturally, it was a jet-black limousine with small flags mounted over each headlamp, the symbols of Kaujeua's privilege and status. Standing in the church's shade, Acosta watched it stop, a husky escort leaping out to open his passenger's door.

Kaujeua took his time emerging from the limousine, smoothing the jacket of his shiny suit, pretending that he didn't see Acosta for a moment, then proceeding toward the church alone. His lips drooped in a disapproving frown.

"I don't like being summoned," he announced, when he was close enough to speak without raising his voice. "If you have business to discuss, Captain—"

"*Me,* summon *you?*" Acosta interrupted him. "Your aide called me, demanding that I meet you here, of all places, and now you turn up late. I don't know what your game is, but—"

"My game?" Kaujeua bristled. "Now, see here—"

And what Acosta saw was the explosion of Kaujeua's skull, before a spray of blood and mangled tissue blinded him. He fell back, gasping, bitter vomit rising in his throat while he clawed at his eyes to clear them.

What in hell—?

*A trap!*

Acosta turned to run, the sunny street still crimson-smeared through blurry eyes. He covered two long strides before the sniper's second bullet found him, putting out the lights.

Job done.

Until next time.

\* \* \* \* \*

# James Axler
# Outlanders®

## GOD WAR

**An epic battle to the finish risks humanity in its cross fire in this latest Outlanders episode!**

A deadly war of the gods has broken out and the bravest of the rebels, Kane, is humanity's last hope to halt it. Ullikummis, a son born of cruelty, has plotted revenge against his father, Enlil, the most sadistic of the Annunaki, a power-hungry alien race. Endgame has finally arrived…but who will be the winner?

*Available in August wherever books are sold.*

# TAKE 'EM FREE

## 2 action-packed novels plus a mystery bonus

## NO RISK
## NO OBLIGATION TO BUY

# JAMES AXLER

# DEATH LANDS®

## Wretched Earth

**There's no place like home. Not anymore.**

A virulent strain of a predark biowep has been unleashed upon the denizens of northern Kansas, turning them into rotting, flesh-eating monsters. Ryan Cawdor and his companions have one shot at beating the hungry rotties: turn the bloodlust of the ville's warring factions away from each other and toward a common enemy. But that means splitting up and surviving — before the real hell is unleashed.

*Available in July wherever books are sold.*

## Don Pendleton
# INCENDIARY DISPATCH

**A power-mad industrialist threatens to drown the world in a sea of oil.**

An embittered Norwegian has promised payback for the oil extracted from his family's territories. Using cell-phone calls, he's triggering hundreds of remote-detonated, devastating incendiaries strategically planted around the world. Nations race to contain massive spills occurring worldwide, and simultaneously Stony Man faces the mother of all do-or-die missions.

# STONY MAN®

*Available in August
wherever books are sold.*